Gone with the Pearls

The Pearl Hotel Cozy
Mystery Series

Book 2

NANCY PENNICK

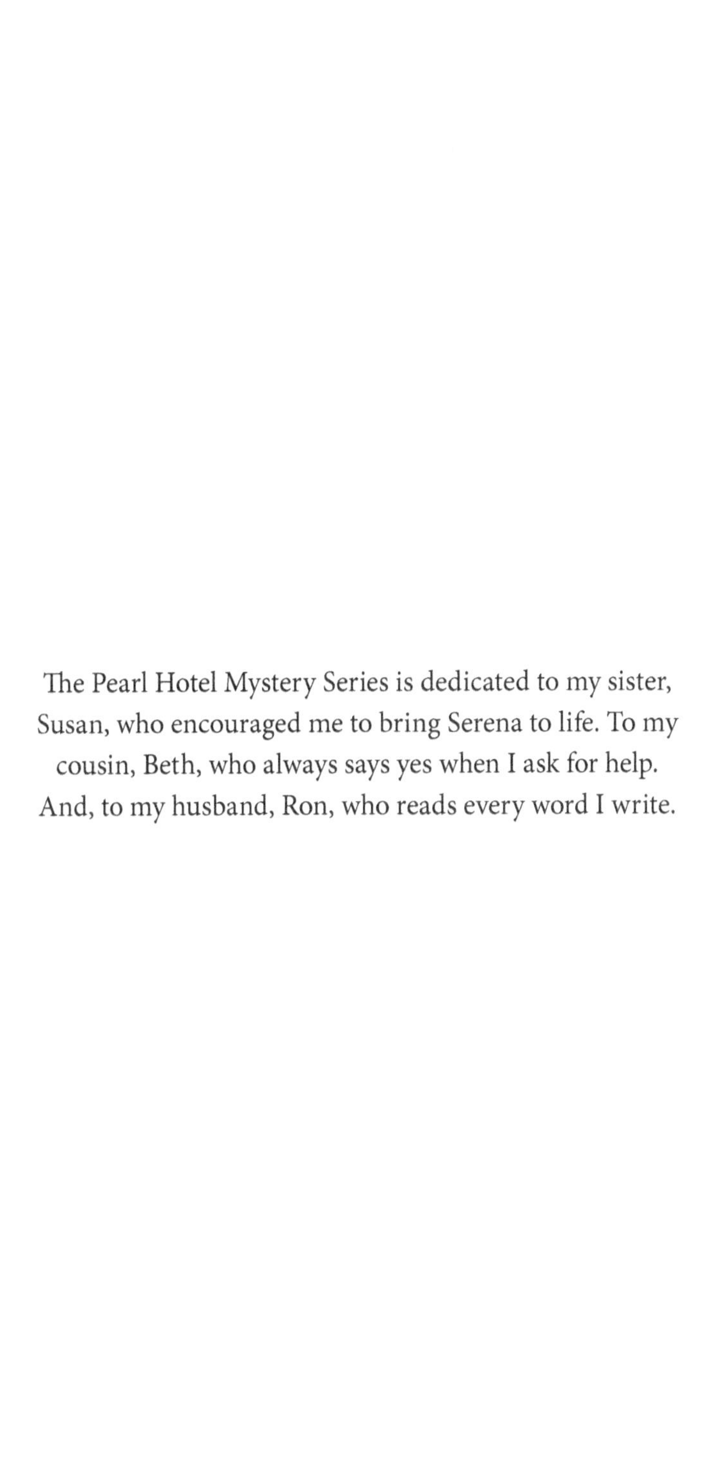

The Pearl Hotel Mystery Series is dedicated to my sister, Susan, who encouraged me to bring Serena to life. To my cousin, Beth, who always says yes when I ask for help. And, to my husband, Ron, who reads every word I write.

Chapter One

"Don't you dare say you have writer's block, Serena Tate," Mia, a dear friend and confidante, teased her.

"I won't." Serena gave her a sheepish grin. "But…"

"But, what?" Lily, another close friend, asked, giving Serena a quizzical look.

"Well…"

"Hello, everyone. I'm delighted you're here." A voice behind Serena greeted the women. She instantly knew who spoke to them. "Nina, won't you join us?" she asked.

"Thank you, Serena." Nina dipped her head.

Nina Takeda, an impressive woman in her mid-seventies, took a seat at the table. She owned The Pearl Hotel, Serena's home away from home, and commanded attention in any room, despite her height of five feet and one inch. Her chignon bun appeared neat, and she never had a hair out of place. With a gift for fashion, Nina always looked as if she'd stepped off a runway. She had her nails done to perfection, never a chip or the wrong color.

Serena smiled at her friends. Mia, a well-known fashion designer, and Lily, a tech wizard, held a special place in her heart. By the similar expressions on their faces, the women also braced themselves for Nina's news.

"I have an announcement," Nina declared. "You are going to love it." She faced her granddaughter. "Mia, I plan to host my sorority's reunion to coincide with your charity fashion event at the hotel. These women can be quite generous." She winked. "I can't wait for the girls to meet you."

"Grandmother, what a surprise," Mia said, placing her hand on her chest. "I've never seen you this excited."

"You have."

"Haven't." Serena supported her friend.

"Serena," Nina said in an exasperated voice. "I am fun."

Lily, who'd stayed silent, said, "Of course you are, Nina. Most times we meet, we need to discuss something serious. Tell us what's made you so cheerful."

"You got part of the word, Lily." Nina smiled. "Cheerleading."

"Grandmother," Mia said and took her hand. "We need more information."

"Let's order before I begin," Nina answered. She lifted a hand, and before Serena blinked, a server arrived at the table. "Could you bring us high tea, Jun? Extra everything, especially the almond cookies Serena likes."

"Certainly, Mrs. Takeda." Jun gave a slight bow.

Serena soaked in her surroundings as she studied the tearoom's atmosphere. The moss green walls had perfectly spaced cherry wood faux windows. Translucent white paper filled the window's square spaces. Matching rectangular lanterns sat in the middle of each guest's table. The designers had chosen seating from the same rich-colored wood, which cast a reddish glow. They'd set lifelike cherry blossom trees against the walls and in strategic corners. Vertical wood beams, with gold calligraphy designs dancing down their centers, created a feeling of being transported to another time or place.

The acclaimed Pearl Hotel provided their guests with a five-star experience. The gardens greeted people as soon as they walked into the main entrance. Stepping through a red Torii gate, they would find a tearoom, sushi restaurant, clothing and gift shops nestled within an authentic Japanese setting. Serena's beloved pond and its stunning fountain sat in the center of the gardens. This magnificent setting helped The Pearl secure a place as one of San Francisco's top ten attractions.

Less than a year ago, Serena had worked two jobs, one in a boring office and the other as a part-time rideshare driver. *Because of the second job, I met Mia. Talk about fate.* She'd helped her passenger escape a difficult situation, and since Serena dreamed of becoming an author, the narrative had fallen into her lap. She and Mia became friends, and Serena had asked permission to write a fictional story based on Mia's actual experience. After reading the first draft, Mia had given her approval.

To her surprise, Serena's novel, *Marry Me Never*, became a bestseller. She had quit her office job but kept the other. Chauffeuring people around the city seemed to fit her personality. She prided herself on the ability to judge their character, and it helped her writing. A notebook always traveled with her, and on the day she had befriended Mia, she hurriedly wrote what she'd learned inside her treasured journal.

A few months before, Serena and Mia had celebrated the book's success in the tearoom. She had wanted to express her gratitude and said to her friend, "Without you and this hotel, I wouldn't have completed the book, let alone written it."

Mia had insisted Serena wrote the story without her help, but Serena countered with her best argument. An exceptional Black woman, who'd just turned forty, needed to meet this outstanding Japanese woman to write the novel. *You, Mia. I wouldn't be here without you.*

"Serena?" Nina asked. "Are you listening? It appears you are in another world."

"Sorry." Serena shook her head. "I was daydreaming."

"I am glad you are back." Nina smiled. "I asked if you would consider giving a book talk for my friends. They're dying to meet you. We will have high tea in the private party room while you speak."

"They're coming for Mia's fashion show in July, correct?"

"Yes, for a long weekend. Friday to Sunday. They want to keep busy, and since I'm in charge, they trust me to schedule stimulating and entertaining events."

"Grandmother," Mia said, looking at her over the top of her teacup. "You promised to tell us about cheerleading."

"Oh, that. It was so long ago." Nina waved her hand. "I cheered in high school and college. My university sisters and I bonded during those years, but as time passed, we lost touch. One girl suggested we meet every five years to keep the friendship alive."

"I thought it was a sorority reunion," Mia said, setting her cup in the saucer.

"We were in the same sorority, my dear, so we call our gatherings sorority reunions. Cheerleader reunion doesn't have quite the same ring to it and sounds a bit immature."

To keep from laughing, Serena bit her lip so hard she thought it might bleed. *Is this our Nina? The matriarch of the Takeda family, owner of The Pearl Hotel, and Take no Prisoners Nina?* She couldn't make eye contact with Lily or Mia, knowing they'd burst into laughter.

"The last time you met in person was five years ago," Lily replied. "Do you ever see your friends outside these gatherings?"

"Yes, for the occasional wedding or funeral. We live in different parts of the country and the world, so we set up a group text. The last address for Nanette and Suzanne Gilbert was somewhere in the south of France. Suzanne is a year older than Nanette, and they've done most things together all their lives. I am not surprised they are both residing there."

"Whoa." Lily glanced at Serena, looking over the top of her tortoise-shell glasses.

Although Lily said she highlighted her mousy brown hair to give it some wanted flair, she didn't need to do a thing to make herself shine brighter. Her personality won everyone over. She had deftly pulled her hair into a high ponytail, emphasizing her lovely, oval-shaped face and perfectly proportioned lips. She was quite the beauty.

"Sounds like your friends have money," Lily said.

"Suzanne and Nanette come from Gilbert money. You might not recognize the name, but when I was young, they were well known. Like the New York Astors or the Vanderbilts of the Gilded Age." Nina checked for confirmation.

"I've read about the Astors and Vanderbilts, Nina," Lily answered. "Many books I've read took place in that time period, and some character always mentions the families."

"Well, then, I shall continue," Nina said. "The girls' father had stakes in some of the world's most significant oil and steel corporations. He invested well and left his daughters a considerable fortune. Don't judge them. Suzanne and Nanette are philanthropic, giving to many charities. The girls even started their own foundation. They build schools where needed, no matter the country."

Lily rested her arms on the table and leaned toward Nina. "Did they ever marry?" she asked in a quiet voice.

"Oh, yes. Suzanne divorced her three husbands while Nanette's second husband passed away four years ago. The couple had lived in New York City, so Nanette needed a change of scenery. That's when Suzanne suggested the south of France."

"You never told me about this fascinating group of women," Mia exclaimed. "Why not?"

"I have an image to protect, Granddaughter." Nina smiled. "It wasn't a secret. I always let the family know when I'd be gone for the weekend."

"Even Grandfather?" Mia raised a brow.

"Yes, Kal knows all the girls. We met at the university. He was quite popular, especially during basketball season."

"Granddad played basketball?"

Mia's expression was priceless, which made Serena bite her lip with force. *I can't take much more!*

"Yes, he was a successful player, but at six feet one and a half inches, his career ended in college."

"Wait." Lily held her hand up like a stop sign. "I figured it out. You cheered at Kal's games. That's how you met."

"Yes, I first saw Kal at a basketball game. We all got to know him since we cheered at every contest. Everyone loved Kal."

"That's how you met Grandfather?" Mia exclaimed. "I never knew."

"Mia, I'm sure we've told you the story." Nina appeared stunned.

Serena sided with Mia. This information might surprise several people beyond those seated at the table. She'd love to know which family members had heard tales of Nina the cheerleader. *None, if I had to guess.* Still, she wanted to hear more.

"Who else will come?" Serena asked, reaching for her favorite cucumber and cream cheese petite sandwich.

"Too many to name in one sitting," Nina answered. "I'll share a profile on each one before they arrive. For now, I have business to complete." She held up her phone, showing she'd gotten a text.

"Tell us about one more person before you leave," Serena begged.

"Hmm, I see you have writer's block again," Nina stated.

"I don't." Serena rested her head on her fist. "Okay. I do."

"I knew it! Too busy with Jack?" Lily teased.

"Jack is in LA," Serena replied. "He had a family emergency, remember? A fire nearly destroyed his parents' home."

"I know, and I'm sorry, Serena," Lily said. "Gabe and I offered to help, but Jack is stubborn."

"Tell me about it." Serena rolled her eyes. "I wanted to go with him, but Jack insisted I stay with the girls. They're headed off to college in the fall, and Jack said I should spend as much time as I can with them before they leave."

"Ever thoughtful," Mia replied. "He won't accept help from any of us, but if I know Granddad, he'll do something."

Nina pushed back her chair, but Mia put her hand on her grandmother's arm. "Please, one more story?"

"Fine." Nina returned to her seat. "I'll give you two." She smiled. "Beth Olson and Linda Gordon. The nicest of the bunch. Linda married well and lives outside of Columbus, Ohio. She took care of us throughout our college years. Sometimes we teased her and called her mom. She did most of the cooking at the sorority house and organized weekly cleanings."

"Wow. Could you send her to my house?" Serena joked.

"I wish." Nina chuckled. "Our other sweet cheerleader is Beth Olson. She moved to Chicago, where she met her husband. She loved children and taught school for thirty years. Her husband was a media mogul who owned many Chicago radio stations besides other endeavors in that field."

"Is her husband still with us?" Lily asked.

"No, he died in January. I attended the funeral and saw all the girls, except Linda. She couldn't make the trip. While there, I discovered most had read your book, Serena. They were dying to meet you."

"Could you stop using the word dying?" Serena shuddered. "Once was enough this year." Serena recalled Mia's fashion event at The Pearl in February. Someone had drugged a famous supermodel, causing her to fall during the show, which was the intention, but they used too much of the substance. The model overdosed and died.

"I'm sorry, my child, I didn't mean to bring up painful memories."

My child. Serena embraced the words. When Serena first came to The Pearl, anxious to work on her first novel, Nina warmly accepted her into the family. "You didn't upset me," Serena answered. "I know it's just an expression."

"You described four friends, Grandmother. Can you tell us how many cheerleaders are left?" Mia asked.

"Five remain, but it's time to take my leave." Nina stood and brushed the front of her skirt. "Let's reconvene, same time, same place tomorrow."

Serena watched over her shoulder as Nina leisurely moved through the room, acknowledging servers with their hands full of trays or carrying teapots. Others, who didn't, got a pat on the shoulder or a quick chat. Once she left the tearoom, Serena faced her friends. "Oh my gosh, I couldn't look at either of you. Nina was a cheerleader?"

"I never knew." Mia giggled. "And I'm her granddaughter!"

"A secret life?" Lily wiggled her eyebrows.

Serena held up her pointer finger. "It makes sense. She had to keep her past a secret. Think. Nina has a reputation to uphold." She tapped her chin. "Still, I'd love to see a framed photo in her office wearing the outfit."

Lily chuckled. "One of the entire team, too. I love names from decades past. But the Gilbert family outdid themselves with Suzanne and Nanette. You'd think they were from France."

"I loved her stories," Serena said. "Perhaps it will help me…"

"With your new book?" Mia and Lily spoke in unison.

Serena narrowed her eyes, giving them an icy stare.

"Seriously." Lily covered Serena's hand with her own. "Your publisher hasn't released your second book yet. *High Heels and High Stakes* won't come out until fall. Are they pressuring you for a third?"

Serena hung her head. "No. I'm doing it to myself. Creating a storyline for the second book was challenging. I decided to get a head start on the next one."

"I don't want a repeat performance of what happened this winter but perhaps these women are the inspiration you need," Mia said. "I bet they have quite the personalities."

"Maybe." Serena drained her teacup and returned it to the saucer. "Time to go to my office and meditate."

"Or to the pond," Lily said. "To speak with Samurai?"

"I've checked the fish in the pond and have never seen a red koi with white fins and tail," Mia responded.

"With a white underbelly," Serena added. "Trust me. He's there."

"Are you sure?" Mia closed one eye.

"Ask Nina. She's seen him." Serena wrinkled her nose at her friend.

"Maybe I'll come with you," Mia said.

"He won't come to the surface." Serena shook her head. "I tried to introduce him to Jack, but Sam never appeared."

"So, he is a magical fish," Lily said. "One only you and Nina can see."

Serena lifted her shoulder. "Perhaps."

Chapter Two

Serena rested her arms on the fence railing and gazed into the pond. Within seconds, Samurai surfaced, beaming at her. "I know what you're thinking," Serena pointed at him. "Things are too quiet around here. Not for long, though. Have you heard Nina's news?" She pretended to shake imaginary pompoms.

Samurai swam in a circle, dove into the water and popped up his head. Serena and Sam had a code. Heads, for yes. Tails for no. "Of course, you already know. Should be interesting, right? A bunch of rich women in their mid-seventies congregating for a cheerleading reunion. Excuse me." She cleared her throat. "A sorority reunion."

The fish opened and closed his mouth a few times as if he laughed at her joke. "You get me, Sam." Serena made a sound through her lips. "On to another subject. Should I call Jack? I haven't heard from him in two days."

Serena had never seen Jack, a security guard at The Pearl, until last winter. He had also worked part-time for the San Francisco police department, and they assigned him the model's murder case. *Now, because of me, you lost that job. You loved being a detective.* She tilted her head. "But you act like you don't care."

The red and white koi swam in circles until Serena said, "Not you, Sam. I was thinking aloud."

During her first encounter with Jack, Serena had fallen hard and fast. When she gazed into his rich brown eyes, she felt a connection. Needing more information on the man, she promptly went to Mia. "I grilled the woman," Serena chuckled as she recalled the conversation.

"The security guy at the dressing room door. Who is he?"

"You mean Jack?"

"I didn't look at his nametag."

"He probably wasn't wearing one." Mia smiled. "Jack Ando works security at The Pearl. He was my grandfather's bodyguard for ten years while he lived in LA. When Grandmother and Grandfather reunited, Granddad moved back here and brought Jack with him."

"He's Asian?"

"Japanese, yes."

"Age?"

"Forty-five?" Mia lifted her shoulder and grimaced.

"Married?"

"For a short time in his twenties."

"So, kids."

"No." Mia tilted her head. "Hey, wait a minute. Does someone have a crush?"

"I saw him for two seconds, but yes. What else can you tell me?"

"Not much. I am not a matchmaker or know much about those dating sites, Serena. You'd have to check and see if Jack's on one."

"Okay, answer this. Does he have a girlfriend?"

Serena clapped her hands, letting go of the memory. "No, he didn't have a partner."

Their meeting had been unconventional. Serena, a suspect, and Jack as the interrogator. She'd instantly fallen for him. Serena credited her winning personality for breaking down Jack's barriers. He finally admitted his feelings for her, and they agreed to take things slow.

Serena stared at Sam, lazily swimming in circles. "You're waiting for a treat, aren't you?" She dug in her purse for the plastic bag filled with honey oat cereal. Nina had schooled her on what koi eat and this was a favorite.

"You want some?" Serena shook the bag. "First, you need to answer my question. Should I call Jack? He's busy, but it's been two days," she moaned.

Sam swam underwater for a while, then lifted his head above the surface. He blinked as if he felt her anxiety over what to do. Serena headed for a bench to think. She had so much on her mind. The girls had to shop and prepare for college, and her publisher chose a fall release date for her book. Throw in an ex-husband, who they'd seen a few times a year until now and her life became overwhelming.

Suddenly, Justice wanted to be part of their lives again. Serena never trusted his motives since he only showed interest after her book's success, and the girls had walked in Mia's fashion show. She placed her head in her hands and took a few deep breaths.

An arm slipped around Serena's shoulders, and a kind voice said, "Sometimes it gets overwhelming."

"Nina," Serena cried. "How did you find me?"

"It wasn't difficult." Nina tapped Serena's hand. "Look at me. What is wrong?"

"It's nothing. I'm being a baby."

Nina smiled. "A baby?"

"I have everything I want, but I'm still one confused woman. I stress over each decision I make." Serena blew through her lips. "I'm debating if I should call Jack or not."

"Let's start with the confused woman," Nina said. "Puzzles to solve. Chaotic events. Juggling schedules. It is part of life."

"You have it under control," Serena replied. "Look at you. Never a hair out of place."

Nina patted her leg and laughed. "You think I never worry or get confused? You see what I choose to show the world."

"Really? You do an excellent job hiding your emotions."

"In my business, one must." Nina gestured to Serena's purse. "Make the call. What is the worst that can happen?"

"Okay, I will," Serena whispered. "I'm going to Facetime him and must look a mess."

"I'll leave you to it," Nina said, rising from the bench. "I'm here whenever you need me."

I'm always crying on Nina's shoulder. It's time I was there for her. Serena glanced around the gardens. "But how?" She stared at her phone. "By doing something simple. Make the call as she suggested. But first…"

For the summer season, Serena had straightened her hair and wore it in a sleek, high ponytail. It kept her hair from falling in her face while she wrote, and she could effortlessly dress up or down with the style. She dug for her compact to check her makeup. No runny mascara lines and the hot pink blush she'd applied earlier still appeared fresh. She studied her features in the small mirror. Her brown eyes had flecks of gold, which she highlighted with the perfect eyeshadow. She used the best cream for her face, which kept her honey brown skin smooth and silky. Touching her cheek, she said, "Okay. I'm ready."

"Serena?" Jack answered on the third ring.

Her heart raced when she heard his voice. "Hi, Jack. How are things going?"

"I'm helping Mom and Dad with insurance claims. We're shoveling garbage from the house." Jack paused. "Listen to me. What am I saying? I miss you, Serena. You look great."

"It's the reason I called. I wanted to see your handsome face," Serena said. "Although you've got a smudge of dirt or is that soot on your cheek?"

"Do I?" Jack chuckled, rubbing his cheek and making it worse. "How are things at The Pearl?"

"Until today, things have gone smoothly."

"I hear a 'but' in there."

"Hold on. It's coming." Serena repeated Nina's cheerleading story.

"Nina was a cheerleader?"

"See, even you didn't know!" Serena howled, then checked to see if she disturbed anyone.

"I can't picture her." Jack shook his head.

"Nina isn't finished. There's more to tell," Serena said. "I can't wait to hear her stories."

"If all goes well here, I hope to come home next week. I want to be there for Mia's charity fashion show."

"In case something happens?" Serena teased.

"No, I want to see Jade and Jewel walk in the show."

Serena's heart melted, and she longed to say she loved him, but neither had said the "L" word yet. "That's sweet. The twins hoped you'd come back in time. They love you, Jack." *There. I said the word. Love.*

"I love them, too," Jack replied.

If her heart had wings, it would fly. Her boyfriend loved her daughters. Who could ask for more? "They have practiced night and day to the point it is driving Mama and me crazy. Watch this, Grandma. Mom, what do you think about this move?"

"Sounds like you're having fun, Serena. Is Robin finally moved in?"

"It took Mama forever, but yes. I think she's here to stay. You don't mind, do you?"

"Why should I? It's your house."

"You visit a lot."

"Robin has choir practice, bingo, cards. She's a busy woman."

"Yeah, she knows how to leave us alone." Serena smiled, showing her teeth.

"I want to kiss you, Serena," Jack said. "But it will have to wait until I see you in person. In the meantime." He blew her a kiss.

Serena pretended to catch it and giggled. "Are we too old for this?"

"Never," Jack said. "Hey, Dad just came in with the contractor. I don't want to end our conversation, but I must be part of the discussion."

"I understand," Serena answered. "Text or call when you can. See you next week?"

"You bet."

Serena hugged her phone to her body and inhaled deeply. "You're never too old for love, Serena Tate."

* * * *

The next morning, Serena's mom insisted she eat breakfast before leaving the house. "Mama, it's sweet of you, but I'll eat at the tearoom," she had told her. Eager to hear about Nina's friends, she hurried to the garage and drove to the hotel.

After the valet took her car, Serena rushed into The Pearl and speed-walked along the flagstone pathway to the restaurant. As always, Serena paused and breathed in the jasmine-scented air wafting from the lobby. Once inside, the hostess greeted her and escorted her to the Takeda table, a quiet one in the back corner. She handed Serena a menu, and she politely accepted it. "Thanks."

"Serena." Mia came up from behind her, placing her hands on Serena's shoulders. "Are you as surprised as I am?"

"If you mean about Miss Nina, the cheerleader, yes." Serena slid into her chair.

"I couldn't stop thinking about it, and when I told Kade, I thought his eyes would pop from his head." Mia chuckled.

"Another fascinating side to our Nina," Lily said, pulling out her chair to join them. "I think Gabe laughed for five minutes when I told him." She glanced toward the entrance. "Shh! Here she comes."

"Have you ordered?" Nina asked, gracefully slipping into her seat.

"No, we just arrived," Serena answered.

"I ordered oolong for the table," Nina said with a smile and folded her hands. "Where would you like me to begin?"

"You should keep introducing your friends," Mia replied. "Although I'd love to hear some stories about you back in the day."

"All in due time, Granddaughter." Nina tapped her chin. "I told you about Nanette and Suzanne Gilbert, Beth Olson and Linda Gordon."

"Only five left," Serena confirmed. "Please do two people today." She begged.

Jun arrived with the teapots and placed one between Serena and Mia. She set the other by Nina and Lily. "Would you like me to pour?" she asked.

"We're fine, Jun. We'll order now," Nina said.

Once Nina finished, Jun turned to Serena. "The feta cheese, broccoli quiche with cranberry bread. Thanks,

Jun." Her mouth watered after giving her order. Serena loved spending time at the tearoom and would make any excuse to go.

When Jun finished taking their orders and had left, Nina said, "I'll start with some information about the team. Building a human pyramid became one of our signature moves. As the smallest cheerleader, I was always the finishing touch. Two male cheerleaders would boost me right to the top, and I'd stand on the backs of Joan Crawford and Sandra Clark. They were the second row of the pyramid."

"Joan Crawford, the actress?" Lily asked, wrinkling her nose.

"Oh, my goodness, no, she was quite older than us, but our Joan took it in stride. Named after her grandmother, the family didn't think it would matter. She married and became Joan Fields, so it was short-lived."

"If I'm visualizing this correctly," Lily said. "The bottom had four girls, then three, two, one."

"Yes, according to size." Nina nodded. "I always did a flip to dismount. The guys caught me, just in case."

Serena pressed her lips together before glancing Mia's way. "I have a hard time picturing it, Nina," she said. "Any old photos?"

"Somewhere." Nina waved her hand. "There's an old scrapbook."

"Tell us about Sandra and Joan," Mia said, widening her eyes at Serena, giving her a silent signal to stop before she burst into laughter.

"Their friendship remains strong to this day. The two have each other's backs. Not that we all didn't support one another, but they were steadfast."

"Did they marry?" Lily asked.

"Yes, they met their spouses at university. Sandra and Ken lived in England for many years, and Joan married a well-known divorce attorney."

"Where do they live now, Nina?" Serena asked.

"In the LA area. Malibu and Calabasas."

"They live close to you, Nina," Serena replied. "You could take the helicopter and meet for lunch."

"We have busy lives, my dear." Nina smiled, but it didn't reach her eyes.

Is there something she's not telling us? Does Nina truly want to host the reunion? "I understand." Serena nodded. "I can barely keep up with two teens and writing my books."

"Exactly." Nina folded her hands. "I am sorry to say, I won't be able to meet again until next week. The hotel is hosting a large convention this weekend, and I must be available."

"The following weekend is my charity event and your reunion," Mia said. "Will you have time to finish?"

Nina exhaled. "I'll try my best."

"Then tell us about one more cheerleader," Mia begged. "Give us some gossip. These women can't all be saints."

"Why Mia Takeda Philips," Nina laughed. "You surprise me."

"Grandmother, I turned thirty this year. I'm a married woman. I'm not the sweet, innocent girl I once was."

"True." Nina sighed. "Alright. One more. I'll tell you about the bossy one."

"Is she still bossy?" Mia asked, rubbing her hand together.

"Oh, yes." Nina sipped her tea, then held the cup in the air. "Let me tell you about Diane Martin."

Chapter Three

Serena wished she'd brought her notebook. By the tone of Nina's voice, Diane Martin sounded like the dominant member of the group. Perhaps even dictatorial. *Should Diane be a character in my next book?*

"After cheerleading tryouts, the judges selected ten girls." Nina continued her story. "Diane organized a meet-and-greet for the team. She gave us each a gift. Day planners. We could enter upcoming events in the small books. It's something you do on your phone these days." She stirred her tea and smiled at the women.

"I'm sure it helped you remember practice and games times," Lily said.

"It did." Nina nodded. "The girls and I, except a few Diane loyalists, came to dread it. I can still hear her voice. 'Get your planners out and pens ready. I want you to save these dates.' It became more about her and our social lives and less about cheerleading. It was stifling. I couldn't make plans without consulting the darn book. By senior year, I cringed whenever I heard those words."

"Did Diane give you a new planner every year?" Mia asked.

"Oh, yes." Nina laughed. "If we girls didn't live so far from her, she still would."

"Where does Diane live now?" Serena made a quick guess. *Somewhere warm.*

"Naples, Florida. The golf capital of the world," Nina answered. "It's perched on the Gulf of Mexico. A lovely place." She paused. "Diane's father had money, and when she married, Diane and Stan worked for him. When her dad moved the business to Florida from California, they followed. She was Daddy's little girl. He did everything she wanted."

"Which made her demanding and bossy," Lily stated. "Did you ever rebel?"

"No," Nina replied. "I thought I'd only need to tolerate her for a short time. Once college ended, we'd move on. I had no idea I'd still see her."

"Diane is the person who suggested the reunions, isn't she?" Serena tapped the table. "You couldn't say no?"

"Suggested?" Nina lifted her brows. "No, it was more like an order. The others appeared thrilled when she described her idea. How could I be the only dissenter?"

"Grandmother, I'm shocked," Mia said. "You always advocate for yourself and stand up for what you believe in."

"Not with them." Nina dropped her shoulders, looking dejected. "I had no desire to take part in the reunions, and that remains unchanged."

"How long have they gone on?" Serena asked.

"Since we were in our forties. Sandra had returned from London and moved to the LA area where Joan and her husband resided. Joan invited us to her daughter's wedding, hoping we could reconnect. It was the first in-person gathering since college. The reunion idea sprung from that encounter."

"Surely, someone agreed with you," Lily said.

"Sandra and Joan preferred to meet occasionally with no set dates, and I didn't like the idea of reunions with Diane in charge. But we were the minority. Sandra and Joan would never speak up, so they encouraged me to be the spokesperson. How would it look?"

"Like you were the only protester," Serena answered.

"Exactly. The others sided with Diane, while I remained neutral. Since our kids were either in college or capable of staying with family or friends, they believed it was the perfect opportunity for a reunion." Nina grimaced. "Linda worshiped Diane. They stayed in contact after college. Linda mentioned Naples several times during the wedding weekend. It seemed she went for long visits without her husband and loved the idea of coming to girls-only reunions. Beth had a different reason for voting yes. While Diane was not the driving force behind her vote, Beth supported the idea of more frequent gatherings. She missed us."

"What about the famous Suzanne and Nanette?" Serena asked with a sly smile. "I bet they don't put up with Diane's nonsense."

"You are correct, Serena. Our reunions may not have materialized if the sisters had attended the wedding. Both had prior commitments and could not make it. When Diane reached out to them, they assumed the girls, including myself, had given their approval. Knowing my disdain for being micromanaged and Diane ruling our lives, it took them by surprise." Nina paused and poured a cup of tea. "At the first reunion, Suzanne and Nanette pulled me aside, questioning why I supported these gatherings. Upon learning I remained silent during the vote tally and Sandra and Joan only said yes to appease Diane, they realized she had deceived them. But, by the end of the first reunion weekend, we reaffirmed out bond and set a date for the next one."

"See, it worked out," Serena said.

"To a point." Nina shook her head. "We are friends on social media and have a text group now. If you do not acknowledge a picture or post about the Martins, Diane sends a text. 'Did you see such-and-such?' I must post something once a week, or she will contact me. 'Are you alright?'" Nina tapped her forehead. "It's exhausting."

"I had no clue," Mia said. "I can't see a gracious way out of this."

"You're right. I enjoy seeing certain women, but how can I exclude a few? My only hope is…"

"Someone dies?" Serena slapped her hand over her mouth. "I didn't mean it, Nina. I'm sorry."

Nina chuckled. "You are always truthful, my child." She pushed her plate away and stood. "Until next week. I'll save the best for last."

"No-o-o." Mia groaned. "I can't wait."

"You must," Nina said. "I have hotel business which takes precedence over this."

Serena watched Nina leave the tearoom, then said to her friends, "Nina is a complex woman. I never thought she had everyday problems like us. For a minute, I thought I was listening to my teenage daughters."

Lily giggled. "At that age, everyone has drama. I bet we all have tales to tell."

"Which reminds me," Serena said. "I need to get home. Mia, when do you want the girls for rehearsal?"

"Since I can't use the reception hall this weekend, I've got to get in the room tomorrow. The last of the models arrived today. We'll find somewhere else to practice on Saturday and Sunday."

"Is Teddy coming?" Serena asked.

Teddy Lewis, Mia's fashion photographer and Serena's friend, had joined her on the list of suspects in February. They'd bonded, and Serena was determined to prove his innocence once she cleared her name. They promised to stay in touch, and through Mia, it became possible since he was her go-to photographer.

"Teddy arrives next Friday. He's busy with other projects, but he made time for my charity event." Mia shuddered. "I'm nervous. If this doesn't go well, I'll have two strikes against me."

"We won't let that happen," Lily said and faced Serena. "Right?"

"Absolutely. Jack is coming home, too. Everyone is here for you, Mia." Serena reached for Mia's hand, then Lily's. "We're in this together and don't need a murder case to send the P.I.C. signal. We can use it when one of us needs help. Partners in Crime. That's who we are."

"Partners in crime always," Lily whispered.

Mia nodded. "To the end."

* * * *

"Girls? Mama? I'm home." Serena tossed her handbag on the mudroom bench and slipped out of her shoes.

"Mom!" Jade was the first to greet her. "Come into the kitchen. We're entertaining Grandma while she's baking."

"The woman never stops." Serena laughed. "What is she making now?"

"Nothing for us," Jewel answered when Serena entered the kitchen. "Cookies for a bake sale."

Serena absorbed the sights and smells of home. Her daughters had turned eighteen in March, and Robin offered to move in until they left for college. She felt lucky to have a supportive family who loved her unconditionally.

Jade, who'd gotten Justice's handsome looks and rich brown skin tone, had transformed into a model before Serena's eyes. Jewel favored Serena, and for fraternal twins, the two couldn't look more different. Their height, five feet nine inches, was the only thing they had in common. For the life of her, Serena wondered how she produced those two spectacular human beings.

"Come here, you two." Serena held out her arms. Jade and Jewel rushed into her arms, and she embraced them in a warm hug. "Tomorrow you'll come to The Pearl with me. Mia is ready to start rehearsal."

The girls stepped back and danced around the kitchen.

"Not too close to the oven," Robin said, holding up her hands. "You girls be careful."

"We will, Grandma," Jade said, pulling Jewel by the arm to sit at the counter. "What else do you know about the show, Mom?"

"Nothing." Serena shook her head.

"Oh, no." Jewel widened her eyes. "Is Mia ready? What about Jordan? Has he flown in from New York City yet?"

When it came to Jordan Reese, Mia's friend and fashion partner, Serena had her doubts. Sure, he had dived into the reflecting pool to save the model during their fashion show, and Serena commended his bravery, but he didn't seem to contribute equally to their business. Yet Mia always made excuses for him.

Jordan insisted on being called JorDan, emphasis on Dan, for professional purposes only. He thought the JorDan and Mia collection had a sophisticated ring to it. Serena couldn't deny he had talent. He did. Yet, in her opinion, Mia did the bulk of marketing and producing their shows. Sure, she had her husband Kade's help, being a movie producer, among other things, but Jordan hardly lifted a finger.

Serena realized her opinion of the man had influenced the girls, so she said, "Remember, after Jordan and Mia finish their line, Jordan works on the creative side, overseeing the material choices and final product. He must stay in New York until he completes the line. Then, Jordan will pack and ship the clothing to San Francisco."

"Plus, he doesn't want to leave his boyfriend, Carlo," Jade said, making kissing noises. "Why doesn't Carlo come with him?"

"Mia said he's a distraction, so Jordan asked him to remain in New York," Serena answered. "Enough about Jordan. Are you girls excited? And may I suggest an early bedtime? We must arrive on time for rehearsal."

"I'll make breakfast," Robin replied, then rolled her eyes. "For you and me, Serena. I'll lay out two protein bars and water bottles for the girls."

"We'll be in the basement until dinner," Jewel said, as she followed her sister down the stairs.

"Okay, we know where to find you," Serena answered. She put her arm around her mother's shoulders. "Thanks, Mama. You're the best. And think! You'll have the place to yourself tomorrow. Peace and quiet."

"It brings me joy when the house is filled with noise and laughter, Serena. Thank you for inviting me to stay," Robin replied and rubbed her hands together. "I'm eagerly awaiting the fashion show." She glanced at the basement door before speaking in a softer tone. "It was kind of you to include Justice."

"He's their father," Serena answered. "As long as he knows his place, it should be fine."

"I'll monitor his actions, Serena." Robin winked.

"I'm sure you will." Serena returned the wink.

* * * *

After the family had eaten dinner and cleared the table, Jade gave Serena a dramatic look. "Mom, we need to talk."

Serena's heart raced. "What? Did something happen?"

"No, it's nothing bad." Jewel shook her head. "Tell her Jade."

"We received a text from Dad. He's on his way to the house and will arrive in a few minutes."

"Why?" Serena asked. Even though the girls stayed in touch, Serena hadn't spoken with Justice since the girls' birthday in March.

Besides trying to manipulate his way back into their lives last winter, Justice had asked Serena to marry him. She'd finally accepted their relationship had ended six years ago and had no plans to revisit the past. Although he pressed Serena for an answer, she had asked him the million-dollar question. "Do you have a girlfriend?" *His answer was yes!*

"Dad wants his ticket to the fashion show," Jade replied.

"It's still a week away," Serena said. "He could get it anytime."

"Dad said he was in the neighborhood," Jewel answered. "It's not a big deal, is it, Mom?"

"No, not at all." Serena gestured to the mudroom. "Could you get my purse, sweetheart? Tickets are in there. Give it to him at the door. Then Justice can be on his way."

"We already asked him to stay," Jewel said. "We'll go in the basement."

"I can spare some of my cookies." Robin reached for a plastic container.

"Fine." Serena exhaled. *It's my house, but they're adults and I can't always tell them what to do. Plus, they let me know he is coming.* "Grandma and I will stay in the family room. Text if you need me."

The doorbell rang, and Jade rushed to answer. "It's Dad." After a prolonged pause, Serena heard her announce, "Everyone is in the kitchen."

Serena and Justice had met as teens and married young. Serena naively assumed it would last forever. He would stare at her with his seductive brown eyes, and she melted every time. Twenty years later, Serena realized lustful emotions and those beckoning eyes weren't enough to sustain a marriage. The couple had never built a solid foundation, and it crumbled after the girls were born. Justice refused to change his habits or adjust to their new schedule.

Justice stood in the kitchen doorway, wearing a black t-shirt and jeans with canvas flip flops. No one could deny that Justice Tate possessed a rugged, bad-boy charm, which added to his handsome looks. His perfectly trimmed goatee and neatly braided hair looked as if he'd come from the barbershop. Serena checked out his arm muscles, impressed that he stayed in shape. *What am I thinking? Jack is older than Justice and surpasses him in the muscle department. Ooh, I love a man with muscles or is it I love Jack?*

"Serena?" Robin nudged her. "Say hello."

"Hi, Justice." Serena pointed to the basement door. "You know the way." Justice saluted and followed the girls down the stairs. "I forgot to give him the ticket," she said to her mom.

"Leave it on the counter, sweetie, and text the girls," Robin replied. "It's time for my show. Let's see how many questions I can answer tonight."

Serena got so absorbed in her mom's shows, she never heard Justice approach. He cleared his throat, startling her. She placed her hand on her heart. "What is it?"

"I wanted to say goodbye and thank you for the ticket."

"You're welcome."

"You should probably walk him to the door, Serena," Robin said.

"If it makes him leave sooner, okay," Serena mumbled. She'd gotten comfortable on the couch and embellished every move, along with a few huffs and puffs, before standing.

"You didn't need to get up," Justice teased.

"This way." Serena marched him to the front door.

"Hey, before I leave, I want to tell you something."

"I'd rather not hear it."

"How do you know? I haven't told you."

"Fine. As long as you don't mention marriage or propose." Serena grumbled.

"Still not over that?" Justice scratched his chin.

"Did you ever tell your girlfriend you proposed to me?" Serena closed one eye. "I'm surprised you didn't ask for a plus one for the show."

"She'd love to come, but I'm going solo for this one." Justice smiled. "I'm kidding. I don't have a girlfriend."

"Right." Serena folded her arms and tapped her foot. She lifted a hand and motioned to the door. "Here's the exit, in case you need help finding it."

"Come on, Serena, I haven't told you my news," Justice said. "I want to prove I'm not after your money or the girls' future earnings."

"That's big of you."

"Can you be straight with me for one minute?" Justice smiled.

"Okay, tell me your news."

"I got a huge raise and promotion at work. I now manage my department. Can you believe it? After all these years?"

"Yes, you're good at your job. Congratulations." Serena opened the front entrance, feeling a warm breeze through the screen door. "See you next Saturday."

"How about a ride before then?" Justice raised his brows in anticipation.

"On your motorcycle?" Serena shook her head. "I gave that up years ago. Not safe. I'm a mom now."

"Of two adult women, Serena." Justice placed his hands on her cheeks. "Let me remind you of those times." His lips brushed hers.

"Serena?" Jack's voice drifted through the screen door.

Chapter Four

Serena pushed Justice away and pounded his chest with her fists. "You've got to stop doing that." Her heart raced, not wanting to see Jack's expression.

"It's Security Guard," Justice casually said, tilting his head toward Jack. "Doing night rounds, officer?"

Serena opened the screen door and shoved Justice onto the porch. "Goodbye, Justice."

Jack turned to follow, and Serena called to him. "Don't. You know how he is. If you leave, he'll love it. Kiss me."

"If you ask, I must obey." Jack reversed course, lifting a corner of his mouth.

He came up the two steps leading to the porch and tugged Serena close to his toned body. She felt the beat of his heart and his breath on her neck. His lips brushed against her skin and traveled to her mouth. Her hands went to his face, smoothing her fingers over his cheeks. Jack captured her lips, and they kissed until Serena was certain Justice had driven away.

"You came home early," Serena whispered, trying to catch her breath.

"I wanted to surprise you."

"Sorry about *my* surprise," Serena replied, rolling her eyes. "Justice came over to get his ticket to the fashion show. Mom asked me to escort him to the door, and as usual, Justice attempts to charm me. The funny thing is, I don't think he really wants me."

"I know someone who does." Jack kissed her again. "Let me ask you something. Does he know what I really do?" he asked in a serious voice.

"That you're an ex-Special Opps guy who hunts down bad guys and uses the job as a cover?" Serena shook her head. "Never. You heard him. He thinks you're a security guard."

"Good. Keep it that way."

"Let me look at you," Serena said, stepping back. "It feels like you left months ago."

"It's only been three weeks," Jack replied. "But I'm glad you missed me."

Serena studied Jack intently. He seemed a bit disheveled, sporting a creased shirt and shorts. His customary neat appearance, marked by a clean shave and military-style haircut—long on top, short on the sides— had grown since he'd departed.

Jack pointed at her. "I drove all day to get to you."

"Six hours?"

"Yeah, I didn't stop."

Serena pictured Jack behind the wheel, determined to see her tonight, and when he arrived got an unwanted surprise. "I'm sorry you had to see that," she said, stroking his cheek.

"Would you have told me?" Jack tilted his head.

Serena avoided his eyes. "Probably not."

"Hey." Jack took by her chin and tugged until their eyes met. "Tell me everything. I'm here for you."

"Stop, Jack." Serena waved her hand in front of her face. Tears welled behind her eyes as she said, "I'm grateful for you. You brought something into my life I didn't know was missing." *Kindness. Trust. And most of all, we're a team.* "Want to come in?"

"I better check in at The Pearl. Tiger assigned Mia's event to me. We need to go over details."

"Tiger?"

"I never mentioned him? He's the head of security. That is…" Jack chuckled. "While his wife is on maternity leave."

"Okay, I always wondered who else was involved in your secret society. You vanish into the basement, and who knows what James Bondy activities go on there."

"James Bondy?" Jack laughed, and it made Serena's heart soar. She rarely heard a hardy laugh from him.

"Like in the movies. All the tech stuff they do. You know what I mean." Serena folded her arms. "Stop teasing me."

"After I check in with Tiger and do the James Bondy things," Jack smirked. "I'll go up to my apartment. If you need me, call or text."

"I'll see you tomorrow." Serena stole a kiss.

"Girls excited?"

"Very. I hope and pray nothing goes wrong, Jack."

"It won't."

"Mia's reputation is at stake," Serena said. "I plan to make sure everything goes smoothly."

"I know you will." Jack winked.

* * * *

Following many days of rehearsals, Serena glanced at the calendar once more to confirm the date. *It's Thursday. I need to head to the tearoom to hear Nina's last story. The cheerleaders arrive tomorrow.* "Jade? Jewel?" she called to the girls. "I don't think you need me, right? I'm meeting my friends for tea, then I'll be in my office."

"Okay, Mom, have fun," Jade said, waving at her.

"Serena, give me one minute." Mia gestured to her assistant to take over. "What do you think of the setup?" she asked, catching up to Serena.

"Wonderful," Serena answered. "Great idea to change the runway. The models will walk through the reception hall on the runway, stop in front of the reflecting pool and pose. Next, they turn and proceed down the runway, stepping off to change in the bridal room."

"July weather is perfect for this. We can leave the retractable glass wall open," Mia said. "People can wander through the gardens or enter the reception area. They also can choose to sit inside or outdoors to watch the show."

"It's very inviting," Serena replied. "The summer theme was a simple and elegant idea."

"Thanks." Mia squeezed Serena's arm. "I can't wait to hear Grandmother's story. It's been a week since we last met."

"To top it off, we'll see the girls in person tomorrow." Serena made air quotes when she said 'the girls', then glanced at Mia from the corner of her eye. "Whom do you most want to meet?"

"Suzanne and Nanette Gilbert, of course." Mia laughed, and the sound was light and endearing. Her long, dark hair hung past her shoulders and swayed from one side to the other as they walked. Her chocolate eyes twinkled in the hotel lighting. Serena was happy to see her friend in a good mood.

The pair walked to the back entrance of the indoor gardens. They followed the path which led past a shrine. Decorative before Nina's brother died, it now held Kaito's ashes. "Hey, Kaito." Serena waved as she passed by.

"Do you always greet my great-uncle?"

"Always." Serena smiled.

"Thank you." Mia dipped her head in the shrine's direction. "Great-Uncle."

The women continued to the garden's center and stopped at the koi pond. "Now's your chance, Serena." Mia eyed her suspiciously.

"Why are you giving me that look?" Serena asked. "I have no control over the fish."

"I see." Mia slowly moved her head up and down.

"Okay. Fine," Serena huffed. "Samurai, are you there?" She stood waiting, then said, "Let's go. He must be busy." As they walked away, Serena glanced over her shoulder to see a red head break the water's surface. All she could do was smile.

* * * *

"There you are," Lily said, hopping up to greet her friends. "Nina and I ordered for you. Hope it's alright."

"You know what I like," Serena answered, taking her seat. "Hello, Nina. Nice to see you. How did the convention go?'

"Very well. Thank you for asking."

While Mia poured a cup of tea, she asked, "Are you ready to finish your story, Grandmother?"

"Yes, as promised. But first, enjoy your tea."

"Oh, no, you don't. We can multitask," Mia said with a smile.

"Then I will begin." Nina brought her cup to her lips and sipped. She inhaled the scent and returned the cup to its saucer. "Amber Morelli is the last and most formidable cheerleader. We girls believed her father bought her way onto the team."

"Why?" Lily wrinkled her nose, which made her glasses slide along the bridge.

"Think of the times, Lily," Nina said. "And the last name."

Lily wasted no time in saying, "Ooh. Amber's dad was in the mob?" She widened her eyes and leaned over the table. "Tell us more."

"Her father was the boss. They lived in New York City, but he wanted her to attend school in California, probably for her safety. He visited a few times a semester to check on her."

"Were you scared of him?" Lily asked.

"Actually, he could be kind and polite, but we also saw another side of him, especially if someone crossed him. Amber could behave the same way."

"I hear a story coming," Serena said, rubbing her hands together.

"Yes, Serena, it's quite a story," Nina answered. "Diane and Amber clashed from day one. Or should I say, day two? You see, one girl chosen for the team suddenly dropped out. Her reason remains unknown, and we never crossed paths with her again. Some say she transferred to another college. Amber replaced her. Diane believed Mr. Morelli bribed the coach and said it right to Amber's face." She shook her head. "They never got along and argued over everything. Without Bonnie Urban, the team may not have survived."

"Bonnie Urban? You never mentioned her. What part did she play in the Amber/Diane feud?" Serena asked.

"Bonnie, unlike Amber, was the team's calming voice. She developed a friendship with each of them and could stop Diane and Amber's bickering so we could practice."

"Being a cheerleader wasn't all sweetness and roses, as my mama likes to say," Serena said.

"You're right, Serena. Too many alpha women in one room, I guess. But we also had memorable times." Nina placed a hand on the table. "Now that you've met my teammates, let's go over the weekend schedule. The girls should arrive by noon tomorrow. Serena, I'd like to start the book talk at two p.m. Afterwards, I'll give them a garden tour. I'll serve dinner at seven in the restaurant, then we'll go to the rooftop bar for the evening."

"Saturday afternoon is my charity event," Mia said. "What's next?"

"Dinner at the sushi garden restaurant," Nina answered. "Finally, on Sunday, they can tour the area using a hotel-provided limo."

"Then straight to the airport?" Serena teased.

"If only." Nina laughed. "My reunion motto is one day at a time."

* * * *

Nina and friends arrived at two p.m. sharp the next day. They listened politely while Serena spoke about her writing journey. Some squirmed in their seats, showing their eagerness to socialize. The talk allowed Serena a chance to observe every woman and prepare herself before being thrown to the wolves. *Just a few wolves. Some seem nice.* She smiled when she completed her speech, and the women lightly clapped their hands.

"Thank you, Serena," Nina said, joining her at the podium. "Please feel free to mingle. Girls, introduce yourselves to Serena."

"I feel as if I already know them," Serena said, flinching after she received a subtle poke to the ribs. She faced Nina and whispered, "You described them well."

"They don't know that," Nina whispered back.

"I could pick out Diane and Amber in any crowd," Serena said through her teeth as she kept smiling.

Four words described Diane Martin. Bleach blonde and too tan, which would show the wrinkles in most women her age. But Diane appeared as if she'd had Botox or a recent facelift. Not that Serena cared or judged her for it. She may eventually do the same.

Sandra and Joan stood out as the most natural-looking women, unlike the majority who had undergone cosmetic procedures. Serena thought they exemplified the idea for aging gracefully and embracing their true beauty.

Suzanne, a platinum blonde, and Nanette, who had golden blonde hair, must have found an excellent doctor because they looked younger than the rest, but it appeared more natural.

Nina hadn't prepared Serena for Amber. "Has Amber always had that look?" Serena asked, pivoting away so only Nina could hear.

A padded headband brushed Amber's locks from her face. She'd teased and sprayed the hair at the crown to give it volume. The long tresses reached her shoulders, curling up at the ends.

"She hasn't changed her hairstyle since college and dyes it jet black," Nina answered. "At our age, she should at least go lighter."

"Also, on the eyeliner." Serena chuckled. It felt like she already knew these women. From the corner of her eye, Serena watched Amber head Diane's way. *Are the fireworks going to start already?* She inched closer, curious to hear the exchange.

"Hello, Amber," Diane said in an icy tone.

"Diane." Amber dipped her head. "We'll avoid each other this weekend, as always?"

"If you wish." Diane exhaled. "Don't you think it's silly for two women our age to continue a fifty-year-old feud?"

"It's over fifty years, Diane, and yes, I'm fine with giving you the cold-shoulder. You ruined my life."

"I ruined your life?" Diane's eyes widened. "Are you going there again?"

What does she mean by 'there'? Please keep going. I need to know. Serena surveyed the room for other attentive listeners as she neared the two women. *Where's the one who can break up fights? The mom of the group?*

"I'll always go there," Amber growled. "You think you're the golden girl, don't you, Diane? Maybe you'll get yours this weekend. Not in a good way, just to clarify."

I guess I get the honor of breaking this up. "Ladies," Serena said, smiling at Amber, then Diane. "I am happy to meet you in person. Nina told me so much about you."

"Has she?" Amber sniffed. "The woman has hardly aged a day. She still has the petite figure from college." She raised her hand, placed it by her mouth and said in a stage whisper, "Easy to throw around."

"What Amber means," Diane said. "We chose Nina, being the smallest on the team, for those cheers."

"I was more than capable," Amber replied.

"Not with your body type." Diane narrowed her eyes. She looked at Serena. "Jealousy is Amber's strong suit."

Serena locked eyes with Nina, who stood with a circle of friends. She hoped to convey a silent cry for help. Nina nodded, clasped her hand around a woman's arm and guided her toward them.

"Serena," Nina said. "I want you to meet Linda Gordon." She faced Diane. "You should encourage Linda to move to Naples. She can't stop talking about your lovely home and wonderful weather."

"I have made several attempts," Diane answered. "Linda is actively involved in her community. Family. Friends. Charity work. No matter how hard I try to persuade her, I can't get Linda to budge."

"I know the reason," Amber said. "She's using you, Diane, for a safe place to land when she fights with her husband."

"I do not use her! Diane is my friend." Linda placed her hands on her hips. Her dyed-blonde hair, cut in a longer pixie style, gave her an innocent look. Yet, Serena had learned to listen and not let appearances fool her. "As Diane always says, you're jealous of our friendship."

Serena chose not to get involved, anticipating round two now that Linda had joined the fight.

"Linda and I stay in touch, Diane. She calls me," Amber said in a haughty tone.

"So what? I call Bonnie, Sandra and Joan, too." Linda turned to Diane. "Don't listen to her."

"Don't worry, I'm not. Amber uses me as her scapegoat because she doesn't dare turn her wrath on our precious Nina," Diane answered, flashing a look of disdain at Nina.

"What?" Nina blinked and stepped back. "Don't drag me into this fight."

"Fight?" Bonnie approached and tilted her head. "I believe they are having a discussion, Nina. Why don't we let Diane finish?"

Ooh, Bonnie seems to be aware of the friction between the women. She's siding with Diane. Or maybe Amber? Is she provoking them on purpose? Serena felt protective of Nina and moved closer to her. "What's going on?" she asked. "Nina is your host for the weekend. Why are you attacking her?"

"We're not," Diane answered. "Perhaps it's time the truth comes out."

Chapter Five

Serena noticed that Nanette and Suzanne were nowhere near the chaos and spotted them at a table chatting and sipping tea. *Are they sitting back and enjoying the show?*

Diane stepped up to Nina and grasped both her hands. She spoke to her as if she was a child. "Nina, darling, you've done nothing wrong. You were clueless then, and we've kept this secret from you until today. Amber fell for Kal. She wanted him and went to great lengths to get him to notice her. She said he was the love of her life."

"What?" Nina faced Serena and clasped onto her arm. Serena had never seen her look so vulnerable. "I don't understand."

"Kal never mentioned her?" Bonnie asked. "He came to me, asking for help. Kal felt I could reason with Amber since she listened to me."

"We're sorry, Nina," Joan said, joining the group. "We should have told you. If we did, you might not have broken your wrist."

"You broke your wrist?" Serena asked.

"Yes, at the end of freshman year. Amber's hand slipped as she caught me, and I fell to the floor."

"During a basketball game." Linda smirked. "Get the picture?"

"It was an accident. Amber apologized," Nina said. "Each of us got injured at some point."

"Nina's right. I didn't do it on purpose," Amber replied, folding her arms over her ample chest.

"You did." Linda winced. "I'm tired of covering for you, Amber. You think we're friends, but we're not."

"Well! Isn't this turning out to be the grand weekend?" Amber pointed her finger at Linda. "You just wait. I'll expose you for the fraud you are." She gestured at each woman. "Each one of you will get your turn. You all have secrets." She tossed her head, her hair barely moving, and exited the room.

Suzanne stood and in a calm voice said, "She'll be back. Shall we take the garden tour now?"

⁎ ⁎ ⁎ ⁎

After Mia's successful charity event, Serena took the twins up to her suite at The Pearl. They looked exhausted but protested when she suggested a nap. She stood in the bedroom doorway, smiling at the now-sleeping girls.

Walking out to the sitting area, Serena sat on the sofa and propped her feet on the coffee table. "What a day." She exhaled, making a noise through her lips.

This morning at tea with Lily and Mia, Nina had told them about the rest of yesterday's activities. Amber eventually joined the group for the garden tour, acting as if nothing had happened. Excited to show the girls her living quarters, Nina had given each a key to the floor. Since most wanted to dress for the evening, they'd come at different times. The keys would deactivate upon their arrival. From there, they'd gone to dinner and to the rooftop bar for drinks.

"All is calm," Serena murmured. "I promised to attend tonight's' dinner, so I need to shower and change." Before rising from the sofa, her phone rang. Squinting, she read Nina's name on the screen and answered. "Nina?"

"Serena, come quickly." Nina's voice quivered. "And bring Jack with you. He has a key to the floor. Please don't tell anyone else."

"Are you alright?"

"No."

"Can you be more specific?"

"Amber Morelli is lying face down outside my apartment door with a knife sticking out of her back. It looks like I killed her."

Serena swallowed, taking in the gravity of those words. She inhaled and released the air slowly. "That's specific enough. We'll be right there."

* * * *

Before meeting Jack, Serena dashed off a note to the girls. She knew they could sleep for hours, so she kept it simple. *Something came up. Call or text if you need me.*

Serena jetted down the hall and leaned on the wall by the elevator to wait. The doors slid back, exposing Jack inside the cubicle. She hurried in, and he punched in Nina's floor. They didn't speak but held hands until the elevator stopped. When the doors parted, Serena saw Amber's body lying prone on the floor.

"Where's Nina?" Serena whispered.

"Did you expect her to stay with the body?" Jack lifted one brow.

"Well…no. I don't know." Serena hurried toward Nina's apartment.

"Touch nothing," Jack said, following behind her.

"This isn't my first case," Serena hissed. She stepped over Amber, avoiding the pool of dark liquid which had seeped from her body, to knock on Nina's door.

"Thank goodness you are here," Nina cried, beckoning them inside. "Oh, she's still there. Poor thing." Her hand shook as she brought it to her mouth.

Serena widened her eyes as she looked at Jack. "Where would she go?" She guided Nina to the sofa grateful Nina hadn't heard her comment. "Can I get you some tea? Water?" she asked the shaken woman.

"Tea," Nina whispered. "But don't order it. Make it yourself."

Jack followed Serena into the kitchen. "I called Tiger. He'll be here any minute. We'll need to get the police involved."

Serena filled the kettle with water and put it on the stove. "What about Kal? Where is he?"

"He's away on business."

"How far away? You need to get him back here," Serena whispered.

"He's in New York City," Jack answered. "I'll call him when we're done here."

Serena prepped the tea in a pot, found three teacups and placed them on a tray. "Take this."

"I don't want tea," Jack said under his breath.

"Too bad. You're drinking some with Nina." Serena pressed her lips together. "Tiger? I think I've met him. A good-looking Black man, taller than you, well-built…"

"Alright." Jack held up his hand. "Sounds like you have. Why ask now?"

"It just came to me. That's all." Serena handed the tray to Jack. "Be a gentleman, would you? Pour us some tea."

"Nina," Jack said, setting the tray in front of her. "Can you start from the beginning? Tell me what you remember."

Nina accepted a cup from Jack and took one sip. "Not noticing Amber, I got off the elevator and started down the hall. I'd just finished a call and was placing my phone inside my purse. Imagine my shock when I saw her lying on the floor. I called her name, and Amber didn't move. I ran toward her to offer help."

"You didn't touch her?" Jack asked.

"I know better." Nina narrowed her eyes. "I still held my phone and called Serena. Then I came inside to wait."

"You gave nine keys to the women so they could access the floor. Where are they now?"

Nina pointed to a table near the door. "They placed them there when they arrived. Count. All nine are there."

"Were they deactivated?"

"Of course."

"Tiger will bring the police," Jack said. "Think. Any more information to share before their arrival?"

"That I killed the poor woman?" Nina cried.

"He didn't mean it like that, Nina," Serena said. "Jack has no idea what happened since your friends arrived. He doesn't know Amber dropped you on purpose during a cheer, and you broke your wrist. He wants that type of information."

"Is that enough to suspect me of a crime?" Nina winced.

"No." Serena shook her head. "But don't keep it a secret."

"There is something else." Nina hung her head. "Enough to consider me a suspect."

"What is it?" Serena's voice shook. She wanted to help her friend more than ever. After all Nina had done for Serena, she would throw herself into this case before it started.

"While I waited for you, I wandered through the apartment. Upon entering the bedroom, I found the closet door wide open, a departure from my usual habit of keeping it shut. A sense of unease crept over me, and I felt something was amiss. I ventured inside, only to discover the place in shambles. Someone had strewn my organized shoe boxes across the floor, and the safe lay open, sending shivers down my spine."

"Is anything missing?" Jack asked.

"Yes." Nina dipped her head. "The pearls my father gave me on my twenty-first birthday. Expensive?" She lifted her shoulder. "But not enough to fence for a significant sum. You'd need more jewelry or costly items to receive a huge sum. The pearls were sentimental. Something I wear almost daily, except for this weekend."

"Why aren't you wearing them today?" Serena wrinkled her brow. *Come to think of it, Nina always wears the necklace. Oh! Did she name the hotel after them?*

"The girls used tease me," Nina said. "I wore them senior year of college for special occasions. They called me Daddy's little pearl. I didn't want to hear it this weekend."

Serena felt this group of women grew shadier and cattier by the moment. "You said you had good times with them. All I've heard are mean girl stories."

"You can see why I wanted to keep my distance," Nina said. "While I waited for you, I reflected on our relationships and concluded that any of the girls could kill Amber."

"But the focus is on you, Nina," Jack replied. "From the looks of the crime scene, it appears you caught Amber in the apartment and tried to stop her from taking the pearls. You grabbed the nearest thing, a kitchen knife, and chased her into the hall. It may have been an accident, but you stabbed her in the back. The police will deduce the same thing."

"I did no such thing," Nina stated, folding her arms across her chest. "You know that, Jack."

Serena held up her pointer finger. "We're missing one important fact. If Amber stole the necklace, where are the pearls?"

"In her hand?" Jack walked to the door and opened it. "I don't see them anywhere."

"Under her body?" Serena cringed. "I guess we have to wait for the police."

* * * *

A knock came at the door, and Jack answered. "Hello, Bill," he sneered.

The short, heavy-set officer stepped in front of Jack. "I'm Detective Bill Mitchell with the SFPD. The hotel called the station reporting a murder. No one leaves the premises without my permission. Got it?"

"We don't know if it's a murder yet, Bill," Jack stated.

"Well." Bill hiked up his pants by the belt, and Serena thought a pair of suspenders might help. "One cannot stab themselves in the back. I'd say it's murder."

Serena knew the man well. The department had assigned Detective Bill Mitchell to help Jack with the murder this winter. He tried to take over the investigation several times while he worked with Jack, trying to prove his worth. His hope of a promotion, Serena noticed, hadn't come through, but Bill Mitchell had accomplished one goal. He got Jack to resign from the force. *A story for another day.*

"Mrs. Takeda," Bill said. "Is this your apartment?"

"Yes."

"Is your husband home?"

"Kal is in New York City."

Was anyone in the hall or inside your apartment beside you?" Bill asked.

"No."

Tiger rushed into the apartment. "Sorry, the detective got ahead of me. Nina, you don't need to answer his questions. I called your lawyer. She's on her way."

Serena's heart ached, watching the tough and determined woman shrink into the sofa. *I won't let her give in.* She marched over to where Nina sat and joined her. "We're in this together," she whispered.

"Thank you, my dear." Nina patted her hand. "I told you one day I would need your help. Use your skills." She cocked her head toward the door. "Out there."

"I need permission to leave. You heard the detective," Serena said under her breath.

"Jack," Nina said. "If Serena promises to stay in the hotel, could she leave?"

"Yes." Jack's mouth twitched as if he understood. "Bill?" He turned to the officer.

Bill pointed at Serena. "You're the troublemaker, aren't you, Ms. Tate? It's probably best if you leave. Stay close in case I need to speak with you."

Why I never! Troublemaker? Serena gave Bill her sweetest smile. "Thank you, detective. I'll be in my office."

* * * *

Serena took a detour to check on the girls. *I'm sure they're awake. Two hours have raced by.* She dialed Justice as she walked to her room.

"Serena?" His tone held concern.

"Are you in the hotel, by any chance?" Serena asked.

"Yes, I'm in the bar."

"Drinking?"

"I had a beer and a sandwich while I watched a baseball game."

"Why didn't you go home?"

"I promised the girls I'd take them to dinner. I chose to kill some time here instead of going home and returning."

"Good. Come up to my suite. I'll have them ready to go in a half hour, and you better be sober."

"I am. I switched to sparkling water after I ate. Happy?"

"Very."

"Are you alright?" Justice asked. "You sound…funny."

"Like ha-ha funny?"

"No, as if something's going on. I swear I saw a police car pull up in front of the hotel about an hour ago."

"Not a big deal."

"Or is it?"

"Okay," Serena huffed. "You'll find out soon enough. Do not say a word to anyone. There's been a murder."

"A murder?"

"What did I just say?"

"No one is around me, Serena," Justice said. "Who died? Anyone we know?" He paused. "Don't answer that. If you're already involved, I'm guessing yes. Or maybe you know the killer?"

"Justice, will you please stop?" Serena hissed, opening the door to her suite. "Get up here. I want the girls to leave the hotel. Now." She ended the call before he could say another word.

Serena tiptoed down the hall and peeked into her bedroom. The girls still slept, and she hated to wake them. "Jewel? Jade? Time to get up."

Jade rolled toward her sister. "She's still doing it to us, sis. Using the sweet voice to wake us up. Next, it will be hammer time."

"Are you saying I use a loud voice?" Serena asked. "I don't recall ever using one."

"Oh, yes," Jewel answered. "An earsplitting one. It's like you're pounding our heads with a hammer."

The girls giggled and rolled to their side of the bed. Jade yawned and slid from the mattress while Jewel hopped off her end.

"Is Dad taking you to dinner?" Serena thought she'd check.

"Yeah, we forgot to tell you," Jade answered.

"Not here at the hotel."

"No, why?" Jade gave her a quizzical look.

"Something happened. Am I right?" Jewel asked.

"Yes." Serena nodded. "I texted Grandma, and she'll be home when you get there."

"Did you tell Grandma what happened?" Jewel questioned Serena. "What is it?"

"Sit." Serena pointed to the bed. "You mustn't breathe a word until it becomes public knowledge. It appears that someone murdered one of Nina's friends."

"It happened again?" Jade placed her hand on her forehead. "At least we completed the fashion show before the murder."

"Jade!" Serena wanted to reprimand her but knew she was right.

"Sorry, Mom." Jade hung her head. "You stay at the hotel, and we'll go." She looked up and met Serena's eyes. "Right?"

"Correct. I'm not allowed to leave the hotel," Serena said. "But don't worry, I'm not a suspect this time. Nina is."

"What? Did someone let Mia know?" Jade asked.

In all the chaos, Serena had forgotten about Lily and Mia. *Jack must have called Mia.* "I came straight here from Nina's apartment, so I have no idea."

"Who died?" Jewel spoke in a hushed tone, almost inaudible to Serena.

"Amber Morelli," Serena answered. "The woman with the high hairdo."

"Did her hair flip out at the ends?" Jewel asked. "It was dyed black, if I recall."

"Yes."

"She was nice to me," Jewel said. "Ms. Morelli asked about the outfits I wore and said she planned to give a sizable donation to Mia's charity."

"Was she married, Mom? Kids?" Jade asked.

"No." Serena replied. She had seized every opportunity to ask Nina questions about the women's history.

Nanette Gilbert had one daughter, just like Joan Fields and Bonnie Urban. Sandra Clark had two sons, while Suzanne Gilbert had one. Beth Olson and Linda Gordon had a boy and girl each. Diane Martin had none.

A powerful urge to interview each woman swept over Serena. She needed to discover more about their friendship dynamics, but her girls came first. Seeing them safely on their way was her number one priority.

"Let's get you ready," Serena said. "I need your support, girls, even if it's from a distance." She held out her arms, and the twins rushed to her, hugging Serena tightly.

"You've got this, Mom," Jade said.

"We love you," Jewel added.

"That's all I needed to hear, girls. I'm good to go."

Chapter Six

As she headed for her office, Serena recalled a conversation she'd had with Nina this winter. After the police solved the model murder case, Serena could finally leave the hotel and go home. She contacted the front desk to checkout, and they assured her it wasn't necessary. They said the room now belonged to her. Overwhelmed by Nina's generosity, she had called to say the gift was excessive.

Nina always answered on the first ring and had said, "Hello, Serena. I hope you had a restful night."

"I did, but that's not why I'm calling. It's too much. First, a free office and now a free room?"

"A lifetime free room," Nina had corrected her. "You are one of us, Serena. A granddaughter of my heart. Although." She'd chuckled. "More like a daughter. I'm not that old."

"I'll take either," Serena had said in a lighthearted voice. "But really I can't accept…"

"You can, and you will."

What did Lily say? We're strong women and don't need to listen to anyone, except Nina. "I'll accept your generous offer. I don't know how I'll ever repay you."

"One day I may need you, Serena. When the time arrives, it will be thanks enough."

Serena recalled her heart had raced at those words. "Are you expecting something to happen?" she had asked.

"My goodness, no. Enjoy your breakfast."

Oh, Nina, I can't believe a few months later your words have come true. "Don't worry," Serena said, unlocking her office door. "I'll help you."

Nina had urged Serena to personalize her office space, so she'd feel comfortable writing. Serena only needed to share links with the decorator who was on call to provide help. She had typed 'Colors that help boost productivity' into her search engine and debated over warm gray-beige, dark blue, warm white, earthy green or soft pink. Nina's words had come back to her as she studied the colors. *Make it your own.* Serena settled on coral and peach with white accents.

During the last murder investigation, Serena had rearranged her office to make room for her suspect board. She'd ordered a corkboard, yarn and push pins, printed out pictures of the accused and went to work. She touched the blank board and said, "I'm putting you to work again."

Serena sat at her computer and made quick work of finding photos of the women. She placed Amber in the center with the other nine surrounding her photo. Hands on hips, she studied them, trying to choose who to speak with first. "Today is too soon. The news of Amber's death may not be public yet." She touched her phone screen. "I missed a call from Jack."

Listening to his recorded message, Serena learned the medics had taken Amber's body out a back entrance, followed by Bill Mitchell and Nina. The detective had whisked her friend away to headquarters before anyone knew. "No!" she cried.

"Tiger tried his best to stop him," Jack continued. "But you know Bill."

"I certainly do," Serena growled and spun in her chair to face the board. "If I had to choose this very minute, I'd say Diane did it. She called you out, Diane." She jabbed her finger at the woman's photo. "Amber threatened every woman, as if she possessed secrets against each one of them." She tapped her chin. "That's it. I know who I'll speak with first."

Serena sent a P.I.C. message to Lily and Mia along with, "Breakfast tomorrow." Realizing she hadn't eaten all day, Serena ordered room service and headed for the elevator. Upon entering, a man's voice inquired, "Is there room for one more?"

"Jack!" Serena pushed the button which held the door open. "If I knew I'd see you again, I would have ordered more food."

"Not a problem." Jack held up his phone and called the kitchen, asking to add to Serena's order. He looked at her and said, "I'm beat."

"I am, too. I planned to eat, watch some mindless TV and go to bed."

"Can I join you?" Jack's cheeks flushed pink. "Not the bed part."

"Jack." Serena slipped her hand into his. "We're in our forties. Has taking it slow gone on for too long?"

"No."

The elevator doors slid back, and they walked in silence to her room. Serena picked up on the sudden mood change. "Did I say something wrong, Jack?"

"You said all the right things, Serena." Jack held her door open after she unlocked it.

"Then?"

"I want you to be certain about our relationship. I can't get hurt again."

"I am sure, Jack."

"Justice…"

"Will always be in my life because of the girls."

"It's not that. I can see something between you. A spark."

"A spark? We've known each other for quite some time. That's what you're seeing."

"Are you over him, Serena? Really over him?"

"Yes. I want a life with you." Serena kissed him, but Jack did not respond in kind. She stepped away and asked, "Does this have something to do with the day you came home?" *He saw Justice kiss me, but I didn't kiss him back.*

"Maybe. Can we leave it there for now?" Jack rubbed his forehead.

"Okay, but I'm not done with you, Mr. Ando." Serena teased, hoping to get him out of his grumpy mood.

"I'm sorry," Jack said. "I can't stop thinking about Nina. She's helped so many people and doesn't deserve this."

"Jack, you told me we can't let our emotions influence us when solving a case. We must treat Nina like a suspect until she isn't one."

"Wow. You listened."

"I'm a great listener," Serena said. "Tell me anything, Jack. I'm here for you."

"Thank you." Jack pulled her into his arms and kissed her, just as a knock came at the door, signaling the food's arrival.

"Can we put this on hold until later?" Serena asked.

"Yes," Jack answered. "Happily."

* ** *

Tears streamed down Mia's cheeks. "Grandmother would harm no one."

"She looks guilty as heck," Serena said, shaking her head. "Don't take it the wrong way. She didn't do it. I plan to clear her name if it's the last thing I do."

Lily covered Serena's hand with her own. "I understand. I'll stay in the basement with security until I find something."

"Will Gabe mind if you disappear for a few days?" Serena asked.

"We forgot to tell you, Serena," Mia said. "Gabe and Kade are in LA working on a project. They left this morning."

"Do they know about Nina?"

"Yes," Mia answered. "They'll stay in touch and come home if needed." She glanced at Lily. "She's our tech wizard. If anyone can discover something, Lily will."

"I am going to interview each cheerleader," Serena said. "Jack texted and said they can't leave the hotel until the police solve the case, so I know where to find them."

"I'm working with Grandmother's lawyer," Mia replied. "In fact, I'm leaving for the police station in an hour."

"As usual," Serena said. "Let's stay in touch. We meet here when we can." She eyed the last almond cookie and checked to see if anyone wanted it.

"Go on, Serena," Lily urged. "We know it's your favorite."

"It's hard to eat at a time like this," Serena answered. "But if you insist." She nibbled on the edge of the cookie. "I can't."

"When we solve this case, I'll send two dozen to your office," Mia said. She placed her linen napkin on the table. "I don't want Grandmother to see I was crying. I'm going to fix my face before I go." She came around the table to hug Lily and Serena.

"Tell her we love her," Serena whispered, barely getting the words out.

"I will."

Serena stared at Lily. "Once I talk to the women, we need to meet. I want to use that analytical mind of yours to help sort the information."

"I hope you discover something. We need another suspect...or two." Lily wiped a tear trailing down her cheek. "Other than Nina."

"Stop. I'm going to join you in a minute," Serena said.

Lily and Serena clasped hands and sat quietly. "I wish you luck," Lily whispered.

"And I wish you the same."

Serena and Lily left the tearoom and parted at the pond. Serena wandered up to the railing to watch the koi swim through the clear water. Within a minute, Sam emerged, looking sad.

"I know." Serena frowned. "Nina is not here, and I have no treats. Sorry." Sam shook his head. "Don't be sorry?" The fish swam in circles and popped up his head. "Is that a 'yes, be sorry'?" She pointed at him. "It's so confusing. I don't know what I'm doing, Sam. How do I begin? I never interrogated anyone before."

Two women walked toward Serena and stopped behind her. One checked her phone, then grabbed the other's arm. "Come on. Let's go. Our rideshare is here."

Samurai made loops and circles in the water. Serena stared at the beautiful koi. "Did you arrange that to happen? If so, you're right. I talk to people all the time. It's part of the rideshare job and why I haven't given it up. You reminded me I have the gift of conversation. That's what I'll use. See you later, Sam. I've got a job to do."

The clerk greeted Serena when she reached the front desk. "Hello, Ms. Tate. What can I do for you?"

"Could you ring Suzanne and Nanette Gilbert's suite, please?"

"Of course. Should I leave a message if they are not in their suite?"

"No." Serena shook her head. "Let's hope they are."

* * * *

"The gardens are lovely," Suzanne said, strolling down the flagstone path. She stopped to admire the landscaping while Nanette seemed enthralled with the various pagoda statues. "Tea, you said?" Suzanne asked.

"I wanted a quiet place to speak with you," Serena said. "It's the perfect place."

Serena led the women to the Takeda table in the tearoom's back corner. Nina had it placed so she could see the entire area, yet no other tables surrounded it. The hostess guided them to the table, took their tea orders and said she'd return in a few minutes.

Serena had chosen Nanette and Suzanne as her first interview for one reason. They'd sat back and watched the fireworks on Friday, observing the situation and never getting involved. Serena wanted to know why.

"Tell me your story," Serena said. "Since Suzanne is a year older, why weren't you already a cheerleader?" She faced the woman to gauge her reaction.

Suzanne smiled. "Good question. It's one people ask many times. Why did I wait? Nanette and I wanted to join the team together."

Wow. They do everything as a unit. "How did you know you would make the team?"

"I'd gotten a partial athletic scholarship for cheerleading," Suzanne answered. "I found if I started school spring semester, I could postpone cheering to the following year."

"The college offered me the same deal the following year," Nanette replied.

"You were automatically in." Serena had no idea cheerleaders could earn scholarships.

"We still needed to audition," Nanette said. "We were eighty percent sure we made it, right, Suzanne?"

"I was ninety." Suzanne laughed.

"Did Amber know about the scholarships?" Serena asked.

"Yes, and she didn't like it," Nanette said. "She threatened us all the time. Amber thought we didn't deserve them. She said they should go to deserving students who needed the money."

"How did she threaten you?" Serena wrinkled her nose.

"By exposing us to the public," Suzanne answered. "Amber wanted her father to discuss the matter with the school and insist they revoke our scholarships. She urged him to give the press this headline, 'Rich girls require scholarships to go to college.' She wanted to tell the world and taunted us by saying, 'This could be so humiliating for your father.' Amber hoped to manipulate us, so we'd do what she wanted, but it didn't work. Dad said to stand tall and hold our heads high. We earned those scholarships and the right to cheer."

"Why accept the scholarships?" Serena winced. "In a way, Amber was right. If your parents were rich, why didn't they pay your way?"

"Let me take this one," Nanette said. "First, they were partial scholarships and didn't offer much money. Second, we took the offer because it guaranteed Suzanne and I could cheer together like we had in high school. My father gave generous donations to the university and other charities associated with the school. We felt Amber didn't deserve to know this, and we kept our distance when not cheering. We didn't like her threats but chose to ignore them."

Not a reason to kill her fifty years later. "When you arrived at The Pearl, I noticed you still avoid her," Serena said.

"We've steered clear of her for over fifty years and have enough people to act as buffers." Suzanne leaned back as Jun poured her tea. "Smells divine. Cherry infused?"

The server nodded. "And peach apricot for you?" She asked Nanette.

"My favorite," Nanette answered.

"For Serena, we have the usual. Oolong." The server poured her a cup.

"Don't make me sound boring, Jun," Serena teased. "I might try one of those infused teas and surprise you."

"I will wait for the day." Jun giggled and left the table.

"Why keep coming to these reunions?" Serena asked the women, adding sugar to her tea. "Amber and Diane said the same thing. They planned to avoid each other this weekend."

"We hoped as we aged, things would be different. People would mellow," Suzanne replied. "We enjoy seeing the rest of the women."

"I agree with Suzanne. We love the girls, except for Amber. She could do nasty things to get her way," Nanette said. "You heard she had a crush on Kal?"

"Yes." *Who didn't hear?*

"That's just the beginning," Nanette replied. "Tell her, Suzanne. You heard the fight firsthand."

Suzanne placed her cup in the saucer and said, "Once Amber realized Kal Takeda only had eyes for Nina, she set her sights on another guy. His name? Stan Martin."

Serena widened her eyes. "As in Diane's husband?"

"That's the one." Suzanne scooted closer to the table. "Diane had just begun to date him."

"And Amber slept with him!" Nanette gasped and covered her mouth. "Sorry."

"It's okay," Suzanne answered. "It speeds up the story." She smiled. "At the start of their relationship, Stan would make a date with Diane, then he'd stand her up. Let's say, Amber ambushed him."

"Ooh! I know how," Serena said. "Let me?" She placed her palms together. "Amber checked Diane's day planner."

"Exactly." Nanette giggled. "I shouldn't laugh. It got worse."

"When Diane realized how Amber discovered the time and place of her dates, she hid her book. She and Amber had a huge fight, which I overheard. During their confrontation, Amber announced she was pregnant."

"No!" Serena wrapped her hands around her teacup, shocked by the news.

"She wasn't," Nanette added. "But Amber told her father. He arrived on campus looking for Stan and allegedly had him beaten for refusing to marry Amber. A few days later, Amber said she miscarried." Nanette winked. "After that, Stan completely avoided her and kept the person responsible for the beating a secret. When pressed for an answer, Stan claimed two guys jumped him in the dark." She lifted her shoulder. "He devoted himself to Diane and promised to give her a good life. They dated through college and married a few years after graduation."

"I can see why there's bad blood," Serena said. *If seeing Amber brought up old memories, was it enough to push Diane over the edge?* "How bad was Stan beaten?"

"He almost died." Suzanne glanced at her sister. "We haven't discussed this in a long time."

"It's like we pretend it didn't happen," Nanette said. "Cheerleaders are supposed to be fun people."

"Like Beth," Suzanne said.

"Yeah." Nanette said in a sad voice. "Like Beth."

Chapter Seven

"Would you mind telling me more?" Serena asked. "Beth Olson also had a problem with Amber?"

"We shouldn't speak for her," Nanette said. "Let me invite her to our tea party." She picked up her phone and typed. Within a minute, she had an answer. "She's coming. It won't be long."

After a brief wait, a tall, fit woman in workout clothes approached the table. "I came right away. Sorry about the outfit. I was in the gym." Beth gestured to her clothes. "I'd love to compliment Nina about the facilities, but…" She stared at the floor.

"Please, sit, Beth," Serena said, gesturing to the open chair at the table. "Can I get you some water?"

"Thanks." Beth slid into the seat. "This looks serious," she said. "Is it about Amber? I'll do anything to help Nina. No way did she kill the witch."

What? Did she say, 'witch'? Serena choked on her tea and coughed.

"Are you alright, Serena?" Nanette leaned toward her and patted her on the back.

Serena held up a hand. "Give me a minute." Her eyes met Beth's. "Did you call Amber a witch? You're supposedly the nice one." *Whoops.* "Sorry, Nanette and Suzanne."

"It's okay," Suzanne said. "We know you meant no harm."

"Thanks for the compliment, Serena," Beth replied, tucking a strand of her brunette hair behind her ear. "But I was too nice in college. I befriended Amber without getting to know her. I work out to this day because of what she did to me. Years ago, my therapist suggested I join a gym as an outlet for my anger."

Therapist? Anger? "Could you explain?" Serena asked in a kind voice. "Only if you wish."

"These two." Beth used her thumbs to point at Suzanne and Nanette. "Tried to intervene. They said Amber attempted to manipulate them, and it didn't work, so she moved onto me. I was her puppet by the end of freshman year and needed her approval to feel worthy."

"That's horrible," Serena said.

"Share the worst part." Suzanne gently patted Beth's hand.

"To this day, I blame myself for Stan's beating." Beth hung her head. "Amber couldn't get near Diane's things. I was the one who checked her day planner."

"No-o-o." Serena covered her mouth. "After Stan's beating, did you end the friendship?" she asked.

"I didn't. Amber had cast a spell I couldn't break," Beth answered. "I longed for an escape but couldn't find the door."

"Until graduation," Nanette replied. "Beth stood up to Amber and told her to never contact her again."

"We supported her the best we could," Suzanne added. "But the damage had been done. Beth realized she needed counseling, thank goodness. It was like she'd been in a cult."

"Now that Amber is gone, how do you feel?" Serena asked Beth.

"Relieved." Beth shook her head. "Oh, my. That sounded horrible. I'm sorry her life ended tragically."

"Amber caused drama wherever she went," Suzanne said. "She never found happiness, but as I told her whenever she complained, it starts within. Love yourself. She never could."

"She never talked about her childhood or life in New York City either," Nanette added. "We could only guess what it was like growing up with August Morelli."

"She loved and hated him," Beth whispered. "Remember his visits on campus? Sometimes I went to dinner with them."

"You never told us," Suzanne exclaimed.

"I hardly spoke and quietly ate my spaghetti," Beth finished her water. "Do you mind if we change the topic? It's so depressing. I'd like to order a pot of tea and something sweet."

I bet you want to change the subject, Beth. We were getting too close to the truth. Did you snap this weekend and kill Amber? Serena searched the room until she spotted Jun.

Jun nodded and made her way to the table. "What do you need, Serena?"

"Beth would like to order," Serena answered. Her interrogation had ended. She'd get no more useful information from these women. While Beth ordered, she asked the sisters, "How did your parents choose your names?"

"You wouldn't know them today, but my parents named Suzanne and I after their two favorite actresses. Nanette Fabray and Suzanne Peters." Nanette giggled. "Ever heard of them?"

"No, but I'll look them up," Serena replied. "Ladies." She put her hands on the table, then rose from her seat. "Please stay and order additional food. It's on me. Enjoy."

"You have to leave so soon?" Beth asked. "I just got here."

"Serena is a busy woman," Suzanne said. "She's probably working on her next book. Does it have a title?"

"Not yet," Serena answered with a wink. "You'll be the first to know."

* * * *

Meet me in my office ASAP, Serena typed as she walked through the gardens. When she reached her door, Lily had responded. *Coming right up.*

Serena chuckled. "She's in the basement, as promised." She removed the scarf she kept pinned over her board to keep the contents hidden. "Beth, I'm sorry to say, you and Diane are the first to get the coveted yarn award." She went to her desk and cut two pieces from the ball. She attached one end to their photos and the other to Amber. "I can't determine your guilt, Nanette and Suzanne. If you did it, you'd probably work together, which might be beneficial."

"I can fill in the blank," Lily said, standing in the doorway. "We can take Suzanne and Nanette off the suspect list. They were shopping when the murder took place. After the fashion show, they had a driver take them to an upscale boutique. He returned four hours later, weighed down with their purchases."

"The same time Nina found Amber lying at her front door." Serena tapped their pictures. "Okay, so no yarn for them, but I'm keeping everyone on the board."

"Here's the strange part," Lily continued. "Someone erased the footage from Nina's floor during the time of the murder. We only see Nina entering the apartment, glancing over her shoulder at the dead body."

"Like she was going back inside after she killed her," Serena whispered. "Who has access to the security area?"

"Just security personnel and people who have Nina's permission, like me. I can assure you Nina doesn't invite people to observe the team at work."

"I'm dating Jack, and I never saw the place," Serena said. "But someone got in there, Lily."

"I'm working on it," Lily answered. "The police have finished sweeping the Takeda apartment. They tagged and bagged the evidence. If I remember the narrative correctly, you said Nina had her friends return their keycards when they arrived."

"Yes, I lined them up in a row on a table and counted them. Nine keycards."

"After speaking with the front desk and security, Nina told them not to deactivate until she sent word. She wanted all the keys in her possession before doing so."

"Were they deactivated?'

"Eleven p.m. that same night."

"Did security check them to make sure?"

"No, Bill Mitchell has them at headquarters and won't release them."

"To Jack." Serena pursed her lips. "Am I right?"

"Yep. Boy, that man is stubborn. Bill wants to crack this case since Jack solved the model's murder."

"He still wants a promotion." Serena shook her head. "Which is more important?"

"Or maybe he wants to bring Nina down," Lily said. "He might think she wields excessive influence over the department." She huffed. "She doesn't."

Serena checked the time. "Before I leave, I must tell you what I discovered about Beth Olson," she said. "I really need to get home then."

"I saw Justice leave with the girls earlier," Lily replied. "Was he taking them home?"

"To dinner, then home."

"Okay." Lily settled in on Serena's peach loveseat. "I'm listening."

Serena explained how she'd invited Nanette and Suzanne for tea, and they dropped Beth's name while telling their story. "They said they couldn't speak for her, But Suzanne texted Beth, and she came to the tearoom."

"Do you think they were pointing you towards the killer?" Lily asked, after hearing Beth's history with Amber. "Beth is carrying guilt and emotional baggage from that time. Plus, it sounds like Amber brainwashed her."

"Cheerleading is becoming a backstory," Serena said. "When did they practice or cheer at games? I've heard nothing about it."

"True." Lily tapped her chin. "You need to do more digging. There must be some happy memories. Why else would they hold a reunion every five years?"

"Sandra and Joan are next on my list," Serena replied. "I've asked them to tea tomorrow. I hope they'll give me a different perspective."

Lily checked her watch. "It's past ten. I've kept you from leaving."

"Hope Mama has leftovers. I never ate dinner." Serena smiled.

"Let's meet up tomorrow after you've spoken with Sandra and Joan," Lily said, rising from the sofa. "I'll walk you out."

When they reached the main lobby, Serena turned to Lily. "No need to walk me to the door. I texted the valet, and they're getting my car." She hugged her friend. "Have a good evening."

Serena strolled toward the exit and noticed a frantic woman rushing through the red Torii gate waving her arms. "Serena, I'm glad I caught you."

"Diane?" Serena glanced at her from the corner of her eye. "What can I do for you?"

"Before the girls leave, I want to hold a memorial service for Amber."

What? "When and where do you plan to do this?"

"I've discovered a spot in the gardens for weddings and other small events. It's the perfect place. I would like to schedule the ceremony for tomorrow evening. Since the police have arrested Nina for the crime…poor thing, there's no reason to stay any longer." Diane paused. "Is it possible to get some easels for photos?" she asked.

"I'm not the event planner, but I can speak with her and arrange it," Serena answered.

"Thank you. You've become a good friend. I knew I could count on you." Diane let out a breath. "Once the ceremony ends, we can go home."

"If I'm correct, the police asked you to stay until they finished the investigation," Serena said.

"Yes, but I'm sure they're wrapping things up as we speak."

"You think Nina killed Amber?" Serena choked on the words.

"Don't you? Amber stole her pearls, and Nina chased after her with a kitchen knife to retrieve them. Sounds like a soap opera, doesn't it?"

Are the stolen pearls public knowledge? I need to ask Jack. Serena took a calming breath. "I'd be happy to help." *And keep you here as long as possible.* "What can I do?"

"Don't laugh, but I've kept our uniforms all these years. I'm going to ask the girls to wear them to the memorial. That's why I need the easels. I'm having two huge photos framed. One of Amber and one of the team."

This is getting better by the minute. Serena bit her lip to keep from laughing. "You bring uniforms to every reunion?" She pictured the women ending each gathering in the outfits.

"Oh, no. I called my husband, and he's overnighting them to the hotel. They will be here on time. Trust me. I want the girls to say their goodbyes properly."

"I'm confused," Serena said. "On Friday, you and Amber agreed to avoid each other this weekend."

"Oof." Diane waved her hand. "We always say that and end up getting drunk together." She chuckled, although it sounded forced.

"Anything else you can tell me about Amber?" Serena asked. "For the memorial, of course."

"I'll text you if I think of anything else." Diane seemed to sense she had talked too much. She patted Serena's arm. "Thanks. I'll be in touch."

* * * *

Serena rang Jack from her car. "I'm on my way home, Jack, and there's lots to tell. It's the reason I called. But first, did you find evidence to clear Nina?"

"It may not be much, but what you're doing is a beginning. As we thought, someone wiped the knife clean. No prints on it. I find it strange, but Bill doesn't. He thinks

Nina was being thorough." He made a noise in his throat. "Have you spoken to Lily?"

"Yes, did she tell you about her findings?"

"She did. Again, I find it questionable. Why would Nina wipe the security camera footage but leave some of her entering the apartment? It made her look guilty."

"Lily's working on it," Serena said. "I have another suspect for you." She recapped her day, ending with Diane. "Besides Beth, is Diane on your list, Jack?"

"Yes, but I need additional evidence."

"Okay, I'll see what I can do. Haven't checked yet, but maybe you can answer. Were Nina's pearls reported stolen? I never read the article about her arrest."

"No, we held back that piece of information. We want whoever has them to feel like they got away with it. The killer has no idea if Nina discovered the missing pearls before her arrest."

"Jack!" Serena pulled into her driveway and put the car in park. "Diane *knew*. When we talked, she said someone had stolen Nina's pearls."

"Diane either has them or knows who does, Serena," Jack said. "Good work."

"Am I still an amateur sleuth?"

"You're working your way up the ladder." Jack chuckled.

"I don't think Amber stole the pearls," Serena said in a serious tone.

"I'm starting to believe Amber was an innocent victim and had nothing to do with the crime. In an unexpected twist, she ended up in the wrong place at the right time."

"Here's the million-dollar question," Serena said. "How did Amber and the killer get on Nina's floor? She took the keycards and had them deactivated."

"We're looking into it," Jack said. "As you know…"

"Bill has the cards and won't release them." Serena finished for him.

"We need those cards," Jack said.

"Steal them, Jack. You know where the evidence room is."

"Serena."

"Okay, never mind. You're an honor and duty kind of guy."

"Really."

"Yes, exactly my type of guy. When will I see you?" Serena asked, wishing to see his face and kiss him goodnight.

"Hopefully, tomorrow. I'm at the station in case Nina needs me."

"What about Mia?"

"I sent her home. She can't do anything tonight."

"Neither can you. You should get some rest."

"Not until Nina is free, Serena. She's like my second…"

"Mother," Serena whispered and wiped the tear rolling down her cheek.

Chapter Eight

"How is Nina?" Robin asked while she prepared breakfast.

"I haven't seen her," Serena replied. "She's still at the police station."

"Serena Tate!" Robin put her hand on her hip. "You need to visit her after you eat breakfast." She shook the wooden spoon she held. "I taught you better than that."

"Mama." Serena exhaled. "I'm doing as Nina asked. Investigating. She'd rather have me working than going to the police station. Mia was with her yesterday, and Jack probably slept on a bench in the waiting room all night."

"He's such a dear," Robin said. "Don't let him get away."

"Are you speaking about me?" Justice yawned and stretched his arms over his head. His t-shirt rode up to expose his abs.

"What is *he* doing here?" Fire shot through Serena's veins as she questioned her mother.

"Justice fell asleep on the basement couch. He watched a movie with the girls after he brought them home. They didn't want to wake him and covered him with a blanket."

"Next time," Serena vented. "This is what you do, Mama. You say his name loudly and shake his shoulder until he wakes up. That man can fall asleep anywhere."

"Hey, you know me." Justice chuckled. "Give me a comfy spot, and I'm in dreamland."

"I'll give you dreamland," Serena growled. "Time to go." She tapped the table.

"Can I say goodbye to the girls and thank them for taking care of me?" Justice widened his eyes and stuck out his lower lip.

"No. They're sleeping."

"Let the man eat breakfast before he leaves, Serena." Robin put another plate on the table. "After all, he brought the girls home for you."

"The police ordered me not to leave the hotel, and I didn't get clearance until last night," Serena replied. "Jade and Jewel were my priority. When they said Justice was taking them to dinner, I called him and discovered he was already at the hotel. I wanted the girls out of harm's way. So, thank you, Justice. Now leave."

"Sit, Justice," Robin said. "Eggs are ready. Bacon? Toast?"

"Robin, I miss your cooking. Even breakfast is heaven." Justice took the coffee cup she offered.

"You've always been the charmer." Robin waved her hand at him, but Serena knew she loved the compliment.

To be polite, Serena asked, "Where did you go for dinner?"

"I let the girls pick. I swear it'd be sushi every time we go out."

"That's why I never let them choose." Serena smiled. "Occasionally, it's fine with me…"

"But they'd eat it for breakfast, lunch and dinner." Justice completed the thought.

"Look at you two, finishing each other's sentences," Robin said.

Serena pushed back her chair. "I need to go. Mama, have you seen my journal?"

"Why no, I haven't."

"Could you help me find it?"

"Excuse me, Justice, I'll be back soon." Robin trailed Serena into the mudroom and through the garage door. "Why are we out here?"

"I don't want Justice to hear our conversation," Serena answered. "What are you doing? Trying to get us back together?'

"I'd do no such thing. He's not the right man for you, Serena."

"Then why invite him to breakfast? Say we complete each other sentences?" Serena threw both hands in the air.

"I was making conversation. And Justice did finish…"

"Mama!"

Robin hung her head. "I'm sorry, Serena. You're right. It's fun to have company and cook for people again. Living alone, I rarely did those things. Sure, I have my groups and church, but it's not the same."

Serena hugged her mom. "I'm sorry, Mama. It's just that it's…"

"Justice."

"Hey, you completed my thought." Serena chuckled.

"I should read your mind more carefully, my darling daughter. I only thought of myself and how I was enjoying the conversation."

"You're allowed to enjoy yourself, Mama. Just not with Justice."

"I hear you loud and clear, sweetie. Forgive me?"

"There's nothing to forgive." Serena kissed her mom's cheek. "I'm going to the hotel. I have a meeting with two of Nina's sorority friends."

"Friends?" Robin shook her head. "Those aren't friends. They've done nothing to help Nina. It appears they are more worried about themselves than clearing her name."

"You make a good point, Mama," Serena said. "But think about this. If they help exonerate Nina, suspicion shifts to them."

"They may not want that." Robin cocked her head. "Because one of them did it, and they're letting Nina take the fall."

"Mama! You are now an honorary member of my detective club. That was brilliant."

"Thanks." Robin patted Serena's cheek. "Now go do your job."

* * * *

"Sandra, Joan, thanks for meeting me. I hope you ordered," Serena greeted them. "I'm only having tea. My mom made a huge breakfast."

"We ordered," Sandra answered. "But we don't understand why you want to see us."

"Oh, sorry. Didn't I make it clear? I want to get to know Nina's friends." Serena smiled. "Since she's being held at the police station, I never got to hear about Nina's cheerleading days. Please tell me some stories."

"Not much to tell," Joan said. "We practiced. We cheered."

This is a tough crowd. I'll get straight to the point. "I've spoken with Suzanne, Nanette and Beth."

"You have?" Sandra lifted her brow.

"According to them, everything wasn't sweetness and roses." Serena flinched. "It sounded more like mean girl behavior."

"Did they tell you about my husband?" Sandra asked, her voice tinged with concern.

"No," Serena answered truthfully, although she had the inclination to lie. "Did he do something?"

"Absolutely not. It was the other way around."

Serena shook her head. "I'm not following."

"You said you spoke with Beth," Sandra replied. "What did she say?"

"I don't feel comfortable divulging information someone told me," Serena answered.

"Okay," Sandra said. "Let me ask you a question. Did Beth tell you about her relationship with Amber?"

"Yes."

"Did she talk about Diane's planner?"

"Okay, yes. She helped Amber ambush Stan on his way to meet Diane."

"Phew." Sandra blew through her lips. "Okay, you know. After Stan got the beating of his life, Amber set her sights on my boyfriend Craig."

"Hold on there." Serena put up her hand like a stop signal. "I thought Stan was the love of her life, and before that, Kal Takeda."

"Until Craig was." Sandra rolled her eyes. "Craig and I developed a friendship at the end of sophomore year. Amber never met him until we started school the next fall. She questioned me at length, asking all about him and our relationship status. Whenever Craig came to the house, Amber would appear. I warned him, told him about Stan and he stayed away from her. We officially became a couple that October, and Amber accused me of stealing him away from her."

"Did they ever date?" Serena asked.

"No." Sandra emphatically shook her head. "Craig was polite and spoke with her whenever she interrupted our visits, but that is the extent of their relationship. Christmas, our senior year, Craig asked me to marry him. Amber went ballistic."

"She was jealous," Serena said.

"Probably?" Sandra shrugged her shoulder. "It made no sense she invested her time on someone in a committed relationship despite so many eligible men on campus."

"It seems she wanted what she couldn't have," Serena replied. *Did she take the pearls? Same idea. Amber wanted something that wasn't hers. The pearls represented a father's love.*

Joan, who hadn't spoken, cleared her throat. "Part of that is true, Serena. But Amber had learned at the knee of her father. His motto was 'take what you want by any means necessary'. She even had a gun."

"A gun?" Serena blinked several times. "How do you know?"

"She pulled a gun on me. I didn't know she possessed a weapon until that night."

"*That* night? When did this happen?" Sandra asked, widening her eyes. "You never told me."

"I needed to protect you," Joan answered. "I had enough of her scheming ways and took care of it. That's all you need to know."

"Let me finish my story, Joan. Then perhaps you'll share yours?" Sandra patted Joan's arm, then looked at Serena. "Amber's obsession prompted Craig to consider a job in England. Her father had punished Stan for disrespecting his daughter, and we didn't want a repeat performance. Fearing for Craig's life, I urged him to take the position. Amber overshadowed our lives in London, and we spent a decade away from family and friends to avoid seeing her. We had concerns for our safety, even living abroad. The uncertainty of whether her father had contacts in London added to our apprehensions. As Craig's tenure concluded, Joan reassured me that Amber had transformed, and it would be safe to return home. Can you imagine?"

"Even though you moved to another country, you still thought Amber's dad might find you?" Serena shook her head. "Not a fun way to live." *And now you're on my list.* "Joan, would you like more tea? I can get the server."

"I'm fine, thank you." Joan poured the last of the pot into her cup. "You will be the first to hear this story. I kept the encounter secret for several reasons. Amber being the main one. She claimed she was drunk and barely remembered coming to my room. In fact, she denied it, saying I fabricated the story. Plus…" She sighed. "I didn't want her to retaliate."

"She didn't remember coming to your room?" Serena asked. "Obviously, there is more to the story."

"Oh, yes, Serena, much more. It was such a bizarre tale, I doubted anyone would believe me back then." Joan stirred a teaspoon of sugar into her tea. "It happened during spring semester, senior year. I'd been studying in my room and decided to take a break. Sandra had asked me to be her maid of honor, and I wanted to host the shower. I phoned her mom, and we discussed dates and guests. After ending our conversation, I made notes and a guest list. While I worked, a knock came at my door. I yelled, 'Come in', and Amber entered, closing the door behind her. I remember the creaking sound it made to this day." She shivered. "We'd hardly spoken since she started harassing Sandra and Craig. I was counting the days to graduation."

"I remember Mom telling me you called," Sandra said. "She loved that you reached out to plan the shower."

"Why are you friends with Amber now?" Serena asked. "It sounds like she befriended no one. She seemed to do the opposite. Antagonize everyone."

"In her defense, we do stupid things when we're young. Time has mellowed her," Joan answered. "She never apologized to anyone but did her best to shower us with gifts and compliments. I guess it was her way of saying sorry."

"Please continue with what happened that night," Sandra said. "I need to know."

"Okay." Joan let out a breath. "Amber asked what I was doing, then approached the desk to peer over my shoulder. I could smell alcohol on her breath. When I covered the list with a blank sheet of paper, she got angry. 'Why can't I see?' she asked."

"Amber wasn't on the guest list, was she?" Serena asked.

"Definitely not. Had she'd seen my notes, she would have reached the right conclusion and been furious. I wasn't in the mood for her antics. Besides, it was private and none of her business." Joan glanced at Sandra. "I didn't want you to know this part. I felt something cold and hard against my temple. My mind raced, then I convinced myself it was a metal pen or the end of the letter opener. Amber growled in a low menacing tone, 'Show me the paper.' I hesitated, and she threatened to shoot me. In that instant, I realized she held a gun against my head."

Joan shielded her face with her hands and sobbed. Serena realized Joan had never let herself become emotional over the frightening incident.

Sandra rose from her seat and placed an arm around Joan's shoulders. "It's alright. No need to say anything more. I am sorry you suffered Amber's wrath because of me."

"You aren't to blame, Sandra." Joan sniffed. I want to finish," she said through her tears. She used the linen napkin to dab her face. "Sorry."

"You don't need to apologize," Sandra replied in a soothing tone. "Amber threatened you with a gun. That's awful."

"Back then, would anyone believe me?" Joan shook her head. "Amber would deny she had a gun. She could say I dreamed it. No one would stand up to her. Somehow, I got the courage to push her arm away and stand. 'Go ahead,' I told her. 'Shoot me.' She let out a scream and ran from the room. My entire body shook, and I crawled into bed, making myself as small as possible. All I kept thinking was I could have died over a guest list. Then I congratulated myself. Amber never saw what I had written."

"Why didn't you confide in me?" Sandra asked in a shaky voice. She wiped a tear rolling down her cheek.

"I couldn't. The day after it happened, I went to Amber's room and confronted her. When I repeated the events from her visit, she acted as if I was crazy and claimed she had little memory of the previous night. Then she gave me an icy stare with a warning. 'I hope I don't hear any gossip about this.' I took it as a threat."

One more person to add to the suspect list. Wait until Lily hears their stories. Many motives, but did they possess means and opportunity? I'll work on that later. Serena reached for her phone, pretending she had a message. She typed a quick one to Lily, then said to the women, "I wish I could stay longer but I must get to my office."

"We never talked about Nina," Sandra said. "Are we allowed to visit her?"

"I'm not sure," Serena replied. "Call first." She locked eyes with Joan. "You didn't deserve what happened to you. Thank you for sharing your story."

Chapter Nine

Serena hurried down the garden path to the pond. She needed a minute to gather her thoughts and felt the urge to speak with Samurai. After reaching the railing, his red head appeared within seconds.

"I didn't forget. I brought treats." Rummaging through her purse, she pulled the plastic bag from a pocket. Serena waved it in the air. "See?"

Serena tossed food to the fish, feeding any koi that rose to the surface. She wondered if any drama occurred in the depths of the pond. "I'm sure Samurai keeps you in place." She chuckled as she threw the last of the honey oats to Sam. "What do you think? It's too early to accuse anyone of the crime. I had hoped to eliminate some women after speaking with them, but instead, my list is growing," she groaned.

Sam swam in lazy circles while Serena talked. He came to the edge of the pond and emerged above the water when she finished. "You were thinking, right?" She waited for his nod. "See, even you're confused." She checked the time. "I promised Diane I'd set up the memorial service for tonight. I called the event coordinator, Randi, last night, and she assured me the staff would set up chairs, a podium and easels. I should check the space while I'm still in the gardens. Wish you could come."

Serena headed to the area designated for small events. Due to the high demand for garden weddings, designers had rearranged walls and landscaping to create the venue.

Upon her arrival, Serena was taken aback by the floral arrangements around the podium and the two easels. She counted eight bouquets. *One for each remaining woman.* Walking up to the group picture, she chuckled at how young and vibrant the cheerleaders appeared. She easily recognized the women and lingered when she got to Nina. Fresh faced and smiling, her hair pulled into a ponytail, Serena pictured her performing cheers with the team.

Serena moved on to the more recent photo of Amber, professionally taken with a scenic background. She held a teacup chihuahua in one hand. *What happened to you?* Serena gently touched the picture. After a moment of silence and offering her sympathies, she glanced at her watch.

"Three o'clock? I've got to change and eat dinner. The service starts at seven. I guess it's the cheerleaders and me tonight."

* * * *

Eight women filed into the gardens from shortest to tallest, something they'd always done from their cheerleading days. Sandra led the way, followed by Joan,

Linda, Bonnie, Diane, Suzanne, Nanette and Beth. Serena held her breath so she wouldn't laugh. Being summer, she assumed they had donned their basketball uniform rather than the sweater and skirt usually worn at football games. The sleeveless, two-tone V-neck top bore a large letter on the front. It had a coordinating pleated skirt, which exuded a sense of modesty. The major portion matched one color of the top, while the internal pleats corresponded to the other.

Serena, the sole guest, sat in the back row, reserving the front for the women. Diane headed to the podium while the others filled in the rows. She cleared her throat and smiled at Amber's picture. "We're here today to honor one of our sisters. She could be challenging, but weren't we all?"

Quiet giggles went through the rows of women. Some nodded their heads, while others nudged the person next to them. Serena longed to stand and shout, "After all you told me? Really?", but she stayed seated and silent.

"Since I'm up here, I'll speak first. On the day the team met, we agreed to become sisters. Only we understand the bond and the experiences we shared. We've had good times and celebrated together. When things were bad, we wept in unison."

Serena refrained from rolling her eyes. *Is this the woman whose husband almost died from a beating inflicted by Amber's father? Although, Diane is speaking in general terms. She has said nothing personal about Amber.*

When Serena focused on the podium again, Bonnie stood behind it. *I haven't interviewed her yet. In fact, I must speak with Linda, too.* She'd missed the beginning of Bonnie's speech, but it reminded her of Diane's.

After each woman spoke, Serena wrinkled her brow, trying to make sense of the memorial. *Is this for Amber… or them? They can say they held a memorial in Amber's honor, wore their uniforms and mourned together. Except for Nina. Was it their plan to exclude her and emphasize her guilt?*

Beth spoke last. She concluded with a prayer, then requested a moment of silence. In the distance, Serena heard voices, yet it didn't disturb the quiet. She closed her eyes and asked for help and guidance solving the case.

"Which one of you doll faces killed my Amber?" a gravelly voice broke through the stillness.

Serena flinched as the harsh sound penetrated her thoughts. Opening her eyes, she turned in her seat to find an elderly man sitting in a wheelchair. Impeccably dressed, he sported a designer suit and leather shoes. A few wisps of hair covered his freckled head and his skin sagged past his jawline, giving him a droopy look. Yet, he appeared alert and in charge of his senses. His dark, beady eyes penetrated right through her.

"This is August Morelli," a familiar voice said.

Serena glanced up to see Detective Bill Mitchell leaning on the wheelchair's handles. "Why is he here?" she asked.

"A father has every right to come to his daughter's memorial," Bill answered, nodding at Amber's huge photo. "He flew in from New York City, hoping we'd found the killer."

"I thought you had your person," Diane replied. "Nina Takeda."

August Morelli shook a bony finger at her. "You mean Nina Masuda? She wouldn't hurt a fly."

Great news. He doesn't believe Nina killed Amber. Serena wanted to hug the man, but never would. Despite being in a wheelchair, he looked lethal. "What does that mean?" she asked.

"What Mr. Morelli means," Bill replied. "Is no one is going anywhere. The women must stay until I complete the investigation. You may not leave the building."

"Are you releasing Nina?" Serena asked.

"Not yet."

"You can only hold her for forty-eight hours," Serena said defiantly.

"You're right, Ms. Tate. The hold ends soon, but she's still a person of interest. If you'll excuse us?" The detective bobbed his head and turned the wheelchair toward the exit.

As the detective walked away, Serena noticed two bodyguards trailing after him. *Were they hiding in the bushes?*

Behind her, Serena heard whispers and shuffling of feet. She faced the women and said, "Looks like you'll be here a while. I'll let the front desk know. Where would you like the flowers sent?"

"Give them to a local hospital," Diane answered. "Let someone who's ill enjoy them."

"A wonderful sentiment," Serena said. "I'll happily take care of everything." She wanted the women to depend on her and see her as a friend. "That goes for all of you. This was quite a surprise or did you know Amber's father would come?"

"No." Bonnie shook her head. "I called him the moment we heard about Amber. I thought he was too fragile to travel."

Bonnie has Morelli's number? She and Amber must have stayed in touch. She may have encouraged him to come. Serena smiled. "He appeared fragile. I'm sorry for his loss." She gestured at the women's outfits. "You probably want to change."

"And meet for a drink." Linda stepped forward. "Especially after the night we've had. Rooftop bar, ladies? Serena, you're invited to come."

"I'd love to go, but I have plans," Serena lied.

"Shall we?" Linda asked the women, nodding toward the exit.

As they left the area with Linda in the lead, Serena stopped Bonnie and pulled her aside. "Could we get together tomorrow? I'll be in my office all day."

"I'd love to see your office," Bonnie said. "Perhaps you can sign a book for me."

"Certainly. How does late morning sound?" Serena asked.

"I'll be there."

* * * *

Serena rushed through the hotel corridors, intent on finishing her tasks. Spotting Randi, the events coordinator, in the reception hall, she quickly briefed her on the situation. "You might enjoy this," she said, describing Nina's friends dressed as cheerleaders.

After a shared laugh, Randi offered to donate the flowers since she'd done it on other occasions. Serena couldn't thank her enough and checked the time. *It's past nine p.m. I'll text Mama that I need to stay here for the next few days. So much for spending quality time with the girls.* Mom guilt swept over her, but she knew what the twins would say. "Do what's right. Help Nina."

When she got to the elevators, Serena received a text. "Jack!" She opened the message and read, "Can you come to the tearoom? Important." She wrinkled her nose. "Isn't the tearoom closed? He said it's important, so here I go."

Serena chose the closer entrance and said a quick hello to Nina's brother interned in the shrine. She waved to Samurai as she passed the pond and hurried down the path to the tearoom. Jack waited at the entrance, acknowledging her as soon as he spotted her.

"Jack, is something wrong?" She looked over his shoulder into the dimly lit tearoom.

"For once, no. It's good news, Serena." Jack took her hand and guided her through the room.

The lights became brighter, and Serena gasped with delight. Her favorite person sat at their table wearing an elegant black blouse and not a hair out of place. "Nina!"

Serena rushed toward her, hearing more voices behind her.

"Grandmother!" Mia cried.

"Nina!" Lily exclaimed.

The three women gathered around Nina's chair, trying to hug her all at once.

"Girls, please. Sit." Nina patted each one on the cheek. "I need to breathe."

"Nina, you're home," Serena said in a teary voice, taking a seat next to her.

"Is it really you?" Lily asked, sounding like she'd cry any minute.

Mia refused to release her grandmother's hand. "I'm so happy they released you. You're free and cleared of all charges?"

"Not entirely, my dear."

"They couldn't hold her any longer unless they charged her," Jack said from another table. "And Mr. Morelli insisted."

"I can't leave the hotel," Nina replied. "Bill Mitchell said I'm still a person of interest."

"That man." Serena slapped the table. "Is infuriating."

"No one will dispute that," Lily said.

"Let us not speak of him tonight," Nina responded. "Before I headed to my room, I wanted to see you. Now that I have, I can sleep peacefully." She looked at Jack. "Thank you for getting them here."

Nina rose from her chair and placed her hands on Serena's shoulders. "You did as I asked?"

"Yes." Serena nodded. "Only thing is, I think any of them could have done it. Although I still need to speak with Bonnie and Linda."

"You have done your homework, and I trust you will discover the truth soon." Nina gave her a hug and moved on to Lily and Mia. "I love you all."

As the lights dimmed, Nina seemed to disappear into a dark cloud. "How does she do that?" Serena whispered.

* * * *

Jack walked alongside Serena, listening to her describe the past two days. They headed to her office to discuss and dissect the women's stories in private.

"Oh, Jack, I'm glad you're here," Serena said, unlocking her office door. She removed the scarf from the suspect board and pointed to Bonnie and Linda. "Two to go."

"Let's go over motive once more. Start with them." Jack gestured to Nanette and Suzanne. "You said they were shopping when the culprit killed Amber. They alone bear no grudge against her. I find it suspicious."

"On the first day, I noticed they stayed away from the drama. They said they did the same in college, and I believe them."

"True." Jack nodded. "But there's an outside chance they did it. Keep them on the board."

"Why Jack Ando." Serena touched below her neck. "You approve of my board."

Jack hung his head and said, "It's helpful."

"What did you say? Speak up. I didn't hear you." Serena teased.

"It's a good idea." Jack glanced up and smiled. He touched Sandra's picture. "She has the least motive to commit a crime."

"Moving away from family and friends to protect your husband isn't reason enough? They relocated to another country, Jack, for ten years." Serena shrugged and mulled it over. "You could be right."

"Now, this one." Jack tapped Joan's photo. "Has reason to kill. She did nothing to Amber, yet the woman threatened her with a gun. Joan confronted her, which I consider brave, and Amber denied it happened. Hatred may have built up over the years since they never resolved it."

"Perhaps she had an overwhelming desire to protect them or, at least, Sandra. But don't forget Beth. Amber made her do some nasty things."

"Joan trumps Beth…for now. You still need to speak with Bonnie and Linda." Jack let out a breath. "Can we take a break from this? Come here. I haven't seen you in two days."

Serena gladly slid into his arms. "I missed you, too." She kissed him and felt his hands slide around her back, bringing her close. "Oh, Jack," she whispered. "When will we…"

"Back to work." Jack said in a lighthearted voice.

"Nope. Not this time. Answer the question."

"I don't want to discuss it. I've told you before, I want to make sure you're over…"

"Justice? This is about Justice? Hope many times do I need to tell you? It's over."

"Is it?" Jack couldn't meet her eyes.

"Yes, and I'll prove it by following your rule. We'll take it slow until you can't stand it anymore."

Jack's laughter broke the serious moment. "Oh, Serena, I…" He stopped and turned to the board. "Think we should get back to work."

Chapter Ten

At breakfast the next morning, Serena revealed the stories she'd gathered during Nina's time in jail. She hoped Nina might add some insight into what she had discovered. "Are any of these stories new to you, Nina?" she asked. "Can you add any details?"

"It's the first time I heard Joan's story." Nina's voice trembled as she said, "She suffered in silence." She dabbed her eyes with her linen napkin. "Since graduation was near and her new job took her to another state, perhaps she thought it best to keep quiet."

"Amber threatened her, Grandmother," Mia said. "Why did everyone put up with her behavior?"

"She wasn't going anywhere, Mia. Amber would be our teammate for four years, whether we liked it or not. Her father would see to it. After graduation, I hoped to never see her again." Nina stirred her tea and sighed. "Besides, the girls and I were young and naive. So much drama happened during that time with other sorority sisters, boys, grades and even professors. I think we accepted Amber's behavior as a part of the experience."

"I understand," Lily said. "I had a bully in high school, and no one cared."

"Aww." Mia appeared concerned. "Look at you now, Lily. And where is she?"

"Living a lonely life," Lily replied with a smirk. "But we're not here to discuss *my* problems. I just wanted to point out that bullies exist everywhere, and we accept them until they go too far."

"So true, Lily," Serena said. "We all have stories, I'm sure." She turned to Nina. "Can you tell me more about Suzanne and Nanette? They seem mysterious, and I feel like I'm missing a piece to their puzzle."

"You said they weren't in the hotel when the murder occurred," Nina replied. "And have a chauffeur as their witness. They can't be guilty."

"He wasn't with them every minute," Lily said, shaking her pointer finger. "What if they took a rideshare to the hotel, then back to the boutique the same way? Shopping is their cover story. I'll check rideshare records."

"Jack doesn't want to rule them out, either. He may agree with your assessment," Serena replied. "Suzanne and Nanette may have watched the drama from afar but still witnessed the abuse. If Lily's theory holds true, they might have found Amber with the pearls upon their return to the hotel. They had enough of her and ended it."

Lily raised her hand. "I'll take a closer look at what Nanette and Suzanne actually did that day."

"Okay," Serena answered. "If needed, I'll still talk to them."

"Is there anyone Jack feels is innocent?" Lily asked.

He told me to cross Sandra off the list."

"What about Beth?" Nina asked.

"Jack votes Joan over Beth, but I'm keeping her on the list." Serena put a spoonful of sugar in her tea and reached for another almond cookie. "I hope to finish up with Bonnie this morning and Linda this afternoon. Perhaps I should have a chat with the sisters again." She looked at Nina. "You have some complicated friends."

"I am realizing it," Nina said. "Past events, spread out over my college days, didn't seem so bad. But when we discuss them altogether…?" She shook her head. "Don't get me wrong, Stan's beating was terrible. But since we thought Amber was pregnant, we understood her father's anger. Not the beating, but the anger. Back in those days, the boy married the girl. He refused. When Amber had Beth read Diane's planner, we chalked it up to her being boy crazy. I had no idea the extent of mental abuse Beth received from Amber. And the gun to Joan's head? I just learned of it today."

"Serena," Mia said. "You didn't mention Diane. Have you spoken with her?"

"No, I've gotten enough information without talking to her. If needed, I will. Stan's beating and the unauthorized reading of her day planner are enough to keep her on my suspect board. But the most incriminating evidence against her? She knew the pearls were stolen before it became public." Serena set her napkin on the table. "Now, if you'll excuse me, I must get to my office. The next interview awaits."

* * * *

Determined to speak with Linda today, Serena took advantage of the free time and texted her. Within minutes Linda replied, inviting Serena to meet at the rooftop bar at noon. Pleased with the response, she signed a copy of her book for Bonnie in anticipation of her arrival. Leaving her door ajar, she pretended to be immersed in work on her computer.

"Hello?" A voice interrupted Serena's thoughts.

"Bonnie." Serena spun in her chair. "Please come in." She took the book from the counter. "As promised."

"Thanks." Bonnie spotted the peach loveseat and headed for it. "This is lovely." She rubbed the cushion after taking a seat. "I can only stay a few minutes. Diane has made plans for today."

"Did she give you planners when you arrived?" Serena joked, then realized she didn't know Bonnie well enough to do so. When Bonnie rolled her eyes, Serena felt better.

"How did you know, Serena? Diane thought we'd need them for the weekend. I wouldn't write in mine if she hadn't watched me like a hawk and made sure I did."

Serena chuckled. "You're not a fan of the planner, I take it."

"Or Diane."

"I thought you got along."

"Sure, to a point. Even though she says we're friends, I think of her as a frenemy."

This is getting interesting. "Really?" Serena rocked back in her chair. She had taken an instant liking to Bonnie. The woman spoke openly without an agenda.

"My sole motivation for attending these reunions is to maintain the peace. Amber can easily lose her cool, and Diane makes sure she does. For some reason, they both listened to me."

"Doesn't sound like you enjoy these reunions. How do you have any fun?"

"I manage." Bonnie smiled. "I enjoy seeing the girls, although we need to stop using that word. We're women with our own lives. I enjoy catching up, hearing gossip and having a couple of drinks with the team. We reminisce about the old days, making them sound much better than they were. Then we go home and back to our daily routines."

"Not this time."

"No." Bonnie shook her head. "It's surreal."

"From what I've heard, you never had a problem with Amber," Serena said. "In fact, you said you called her father as soon as you heard of Amber's death. You have his number, so obviously, you were still in contact with Amber and her family."

"You're right. I called Amber's father to tell him she had died. He's my uncle, and she was my cousin. I had to inform the family."

Serena dropped her jaw and couldn't seem to close her mouth. She tried to speak a few times but found no words. *Bonnie is coming off the board. No way would she kill a family member.*

"You probably wonder why we never announced the connection," Bonnie said. "Uncle August, my mom's older brother, wanted to protect her. He encouraged her to seek a life outside the family business in New York City and find a husband elsewhere. Mom did as he asked but stayed close to her favorite brother by settling in the Philadelphia area. We only saw each other during Christmas and important occasions, with Uncle Augie always traveling to visit us. We never ventured into the city. Eventually, as we grew older, I explored New York with my cousin Amber." She paused as if in thought.

"Am I the only one you've told?" Serena asked.

"Yes." Bonnie nodded.

"How did you and Amber end up at a California college when you lived on the east coast?"

"It was my dream to live in California, so I applied to many colleges in the state. One university offered me a chance to try out for their cheer team. I couldn't believe my good fortune and begged my parents to let me go. They held tryouts in spring and again in the summer. My mom and I flew to California in the spring, and to my surprise, I made the team." Bonnie stared at her hands. "My mom had hoped I wouldn't."

"She indulged you but thought nothing would come of it." Serena nodded. "I get it."

"Mom was happy for me but explained they couldn't afford to send me to the school. She thought the trip would satisfy my dream of seeing California."

"But you ended up at the school, along with Amber," Serena said.

"Yes, Uncle Augie generously offered to cover expenses. Amber, who was my age, expressed a desire to join me. We roomed together and relished the college experience. Once we arrived, Amber thought it'd be fun to try out for the cheer team. At first, I was unaware Uncle Augie had bribed the coach to ensure a spot for Amber but eventually discovered the truth along with the others."

"Wow." Serena sat mesmerized in her chair. "That's quite the story. All these years, no one realized you were family?"

"No. Amber and I liked it that way. She said they didn't deserve to know she had the best friend and cousin in the world."

"Obviously, you didn't kill her."

"What? No." Bonnie appeared shaken.

"Who do you think did?" Serena asked.

"Definitely not Nina. If I had to choose, I'd pick Diane."

Oh, no. Jack thinks it's Joan. Now she accuses Diane. What a tangled web we weave.

* * * *

Jack tapped on Serena's open door. "Safe to come in?"

"I'm alone," Serena replied. "But not for long. I'm meeting Linda at the rooftop bar in fifteen minutes."

"Day drinking?"

"Not me." Serena shook her head, recalling a memory.

The first time she'd met Mia, they'd stopped at a bar before Serena drove her home. Mia had a tense encounter with an ex-boyfriend and wanted a drink. Serena agreed to join her, and they bonded over shared interests. Although Mia didn't know, Serena had drunk virgin gin and tonics. So essentially tonic. *A rideshare driver never drinks on the job.* Later, she discovered Mia rarely drank more than one cocktail, and the three she had were unusual. She smiled as she remembered her friend's beautiful dark eyes flashing with anger when she spoke of her ex's arrogance, then ordering another drink.

"Hey, you there?" Jack asked. "You seem miles away."

"I'm back." Serena rose from her computer chair and shut the door. "For privacy." She winked. "There's a problem."

"With us?" Jack widened his eyes.

"No, with the case."

"Oh."

"The list of suspects is growing instead of shrinking."

"You're hoping Linda might help with that."

"How, Jack? You're the expert. What tactics do you use? How can you tell if someone is lying or telling the truth?"

"It's not a science, Serena. You need cold, hard facts, then trust your gut. Don't let your emotions take over." Jack paused in thought before continuing. "Look for signs. Does a person evade a question or change the subject? Watch for body tells. Blinking. Glancing away and not making eye contact."

"Great suggestions." Serena walked closer to him. "What are my eyes saying?"

"That you like me." Jack chuckled.

"Anything else?"

"You want me to kiss you and wish you luck."

"Keep going."

"Serena, come here." Jack slipped his hands around her waist. "I never met anyone like you. Gorgeous, smart and brave."

Tears stung the back of Serena's eyes. "And I met no one as kind, handsome and intelligent as you." She leaned against his muscled chest and gazed up at him. "Let's never change."

"Never." Jack's lips found hers, and they lingered for a moment.

Serena's phone alarm chimed, signaling it was time to leave. "I don't want to go," she said, moving away from the warmth of Jack's body.

"I'm on the clock, so duty calls," Jack replied. "If that helps."

"It does." Serena smiled. "When is your shift over? Can we meet for dinner?"

"I make my own hours," Jack said. "I'll text you after I speak with the maître d." He kissed her once more. "Don't let Linda talk you into having a drink. Detectives need to keep their wits about them."

"So now I'm a detective." Serena placed a hand on her hip. "Thank you, sir."

"You learned a lot on the last case. Don't let it go to your head." Jack waved as he headed for the door.

"Jack?"

He had the door open, but upon hearing his name turned towards her.

"I love to joke and banter with you, but I realize this is serious. I want you to know that."

Jack dipped his head once. "I do."

* * * *

With summer temperatures typically in the high sixties, the rooftop bar offered a pleasurable experience. At times, it could reach eighty, but one could always count on chillier nights. July weather was just as pleasant as other months, although it came with a healthy dose of Bay area fog. Misty mornings were normal from April to October, but the fog usually burned off by the afternoon.

Serena found Linda sitting at a grouping of dark brown rattan furniture sporting beige cushions. The sectional and extra seats surrounded a square glass-top rattan table. A wine bottle with two glasses sat on top.

"A table for two would do," Serena joked as she said adjacent to Linda.

"The others will join us later," Linda said. "It's the reason I chose the rooftop bar. I hope you can stay and visit with the girls."

Bonnie said Diane had made plans for the group. Is this it? "Perhaps." Serena smiled. "Since you can't leave the hotel, I'm glad there's so much for you to do."

"If Diane has her way, we'll experience it all."

I was right. "Bonnie told me you received planners for the weekend. Was this an entry for today?"

"Yes, it's why I chose to meet here and came an hour earlier."

"Great," Serena said, relieved the others wouldn't arrive soon. "Let's chat and get acquainted."

Linda reached for the wine and refilled her glass. "Join me?"

"It's a little too early for me," Serena said, then quickly added. "But please don't stop on my account."

"Don't worry, I won't." Linda waved to the server. "Could you bring my friend a drink?"

"Of course." He turned to Serena and said, "Would you like the usual, Ms. Tate?"

"Yes, thanks, Alex."

"I'm impressed," Linda said, adjusting her sunglasses. "Everyone knows you."

"Not really. When I'm writing, I come up here to think." Serena nodded at Alex when he placed an iced tea in front of her.

"The hotel is like a mini city," Linda replied. "All it needs is a grocery store." She chuckled.

"I'd love to hear your stories from back in the day." Serena stirred her tea with the straw. "Nina said you were the nicest of the bunch."

"That was sweet of her to say."

"They sometimes called you 'mom' because you were always cleaning up after them or cooking."

"Someone had to do it." Linda sounded annoyed.

"Ooh, sorry, bad memory?"

"No, forgive me. I liked a clean house and didn't mind making a few meals." Linda smiled. "They never reciprocated. I would have enjoyed a little pampering." She set her empty glass on the table. "It's one reason I love visiting Diane in Naples. I don't lift a finger. It's truly a vacation."

"Does your husband go with you?" Serena asked, although she knew the answer.

"No, Frank stays home. He doesn't like to travel. Besides, he still works." Linda refilled her glass.

Serena checked the contents of the bottle. *It's almost empty.* "If he doesn't mind, then go ahead and enjoy yourself, right?'

"See, you agree with me." Linda pointed at her, slurring her words. "He drinks. We fight. I go to Florida and come home to a remorseful husband."

Chapter Eleven

Does Linda start the fights on purpose? An excellent excuse to go to Florida alone. "I'm glad it works for you." Serena shifted in her seat and gazed at the reflecting pool. The fountain sprayed water at least ten feet into the air, as if trying to interrupt the peaceful setting. "I'm surprised your husband hasn't retired," she replied, her back slightly turned away from Linda.

"He needs to work. We must keep up with the Joneses, as the saying goes," Linda answered in a light tone. "I still have a job, but let's keep it between us."

Serena changed position and faced Linda. "How can you visit Diane so often?"

"I work from home." Linda lifted a shoulder. "Diane sleeps until ten, so she has no clue what I'm doing. I'm up and at my computer by seven. I take a morning break and join her for coffee in the kitchen, then retreat to my room to catch up on emails. Or so she thinks. It's an excuse so I can resume my work. When I turned seventy, I went to part time and sign off at one p.m."

"Sound like you love your job and couldn't give it up."

"Oh, no. I hate working, but we need the two incomes. Selling the house and downsizing is an option, but what would the girls think?"

"What do you care?" Serena asked. "Nina wouldn't." She sat forward and clasped her hands together. "Speaking of Nina, let me ask you something. Who do you think killed Amber?"

"Quite a subject change." Linda chuckled. "I've been mulling it over for days now. It makes sense to have a partner. I think Nanette and Suzanne did it. They always thought they were better than us with their rich daddy paying their way. They'd go crying to him, and he'd fix everything."

Jealous much? "Nina's dad had money, too."

"She didn't flaunt it like the Gilbert girls. Back in the day, they attempted to get Amber kicked off the team. You see how well that worked." Linda crossed one leg over the other. "They had their choice of husbands. Men lined up to date them."

"I can see why. They're quite attractive."

Linda made a noise in her throat. "Whatever. They never got Amber off the team, and it irks them to this day."

"Not enough to kill Amber," Serena said.

"Oh, you'd be surprised," Linda answered.

"Is there something I should know?" Serena lifted her sunglasses and studied Linda's body language. *She seems relaxed but also drank a bottle of wine. Did it give her the courage to speak against the sisters?*

"Serena!" Diane cried. "So glad you could join us. I wasn't sure you'd come when you didn't answer my text message. You should check your phone more often."

Is she scolding me? "It's a beautiful day," Serena replied. "I had to come."

Alex followed behind Diane, placing water and iced tea pitchers on the table along with eight glasses. He turned to Diane and said, "Three bottles of Chardonnay, correct?"

"Yes, and it looks like we need six glasses."

"Is Nina invited?" Serena asked after Diane chose a seat next to her. She noticed a group of familiar women coming her way, but not one resembled her friend.

"I did, Serena. But you know Nina. She's hard at work and might join us later."

Alex returned as the women settled into their places. "Lunch is on its way," he said to Diane, setting the wine bottles and glasses on the table.

"Diane, you think of everything," Linda said. "I'm starving."

Within minutes, two servers arrived with summer salads adorned with fruit. Serena was surprised to see enough for all. Ready to decline a salad since she hadn't RSVP'd, she gave Diane a questioning look.

"I knew you would come," Diane said with a wave and a smile.

While they ate, Serena took notice of who drank wine or chose water, and which women spoke to each other. Most enjoyed their salads, which Serena thought were expertly prepared, but a few barely ate. *What does it mean? Probably nothing. Or…they think someone poisoned their food? No. Too dramatic.*

Serena's phone pinged, indicating she'd gotten a text. Lily's name popped up on her screen. *Call me.* "If you'll excuse me for a minute, my girls need me." She left the group and walked to the other end of the bar, hitting Lily's number as she went.

"Serena?" Lily sounded excited. "I have something."

"Tell me."

"I went shopping."

"You called to say you went shopping," Serena huffed.

"Not frivolous shopping, my dear friend. I went to the boutique."

"Oh! The one Suzanne and Nanette visited."

"Exactly. And guess what? They were not there the entire time. The women left the shop before Amber was killed and returned an hour and a half later. Sufficient time to do the deed and return to the boutique. They paid for their purchases, then contacted The Pearl's chauffeur to take them to the hotel."

"You were right, Lily. Suzanne and Nanette are now suspects," Serena said. "But it sounds too easy."

"Why? You must get them alone and speak with them. Read their faces. Look into their eyes."

"Should I tell them I know they left the boutique?"

"Yes, let them know we're watching and investigating. Make them nervous."

"Fine."

"You sound disappointed, Serena."

"Not really. We're supposed to be crossing suspects off the list, not adding more."

"I understand, but we must follow our leads. I'll update Mia and get her perspective. I'm not saying they did it, but we need to clear or report them. We need a P.I.C. meeting soon. Dinner?"

"Yes, and you'll let Mia know?"

"Of course. Where are you? I never asked."

"At the rooftop bar, having lunch with the girls."

"I'm rolling my eyes."

"I thought you were." Serena chuckled.

"Are they wearing normal clothes?"

"Normal, as in not cheerleading outfits?"

"Well?"

"They are appropriately dressed, but I discovered Diane is making them use day planners."

"Watch out. If she gives you one, you'll be on the team. Before you know it, she'll fit you for an outfit."

"Please, no." Serena smiled. She had sought a break from those women but could now face them again. "I better go. I'll find an opportunity to talk to the sisters. Hopefully, when I see you, I'll have some answers."

"Good luck."

Serena took a cleansing breath and strolled back to the table, admiring the gardens as she walked along.

"Are your girls okay?" Bonnie asked.

"Yes, thanks for asking. I'm staying at The Pearl for a couple of days, and I forgot to check in with them." The famous mom guilt swept over her. She heard Jack's words in her head, reminding her she only had a few weeks left of quality time with them.

"Are they professional models?" Diane asked. "Given everything that happened, I never had the chance to ask."

"No, although they will love that you thought they were." Serena shook her head. "They start college in a few weeks."

"I'd encourage them to keep modeling," Sandra said. "They looked wonderful on stage."

After discussing her daughters and emphasizing the importance of education, Serena sought an opportunity to speak with the siblings. When Suzanne excused herself to go to the bar, Serena followed. Nanette wasn't far behind. They slid onto stools at the corner. Nanette and Suzanne on one side. Serena adjacent to them.

"I don't like Chardonnay," Nanette said. "Diane assumes it's our drink of choice."

"I'm okay with it, but I thought we'd order something sparkling from the bar," Suzanne said. "Care to join us, Serena?"

"Thanks, but I came to ask for another pitcher of iced tea." Serena shook her empty glass, and the ice cubes hit the sides.

"Let me." Alex approached and took her glass.

"And a pitcher for the table," Serena requested. "Thanks, Alex." She'd make sure he received a large tip from her later.

"Ladies?" Alex faced the sisters when he returned with Serena's tea.

"A fun, sparkling wine," Nanette said. "Surprise us."

After Alex served their drinks, Serena got right to the point. "Who do you think killed Amber? You insinuated Beth did, but you never really said."

"We don't know," Suzanne answered in an icy voice.

"Come on. You must have discussed it." Serena made eye contact with Nanette.

"As Suzanne said, we have no idea." Nanette's voice sounded equally cold. "We trust the police to make the proper arrest."

"So, you weren't accusing Beth?"

"Absolutely not! She's one of her dearest friends. We thought you needed to hear her story so you could learn about Amber's manipulative personality." Nanette stared daggers at Serena.

"Can I ask something?" Serena grimaced. "Does anyone call you Sue and Nan?"

"No!" they exclaimed simultaneously.

"Sorry." Serena held up her hands. "Just asking." She hoped she'd broken the chill she'd caused.

"We despise those names," Suzanne answered.

"You never liked your names?" Serena asked.

"Yes, we like them," Nanette replied. "Not the nicknames."

"Nanette took on anyone in grade school who used them," Suzanne said with a smile.

"You mean fight them?" Serena widened her eyes.

"You bet." Suzanne nodded. "Times were different then."

"As long as the teacher didn't see," Nanette said with sincerity.

Capable of fighting and teaching people lessons. Serena longed for her journal. "Did Amber ever call you…" Serena twirled her finger in the air. "Those names."

"Oh, she tried," Suzanne said, elbowing Nanette. "You showed her."

Whoa. Nanette is the tougher one. "Still hold a grudge?"

"About our names?" Suzanne blew through her lips and waved a hand. "No. It's past history."

"I heard you tried to get Amber off the cheerleading team. You forgot to mention that little detail."

"Who told you that?" Nanette asked.

Serena lifted her shoulder. "One of the women. I forget who."

"An impossible task," Nanette answered. "Especially after Dad learned who her father was. He said it was not a risk worth taking."

"Sounds scary. Did August Morelli threaten you or your dad?" Serena asked.

"I can't recall," Nanette replied. "Maybe?"

Serena faced Suzanne. "What do you remember?"

"Daddy would let nothing happen to us, but I recall a hint of a threat."

"You avoided Amber during your college years but watched from afar, taking notice of her malicious acts." Serena hoped to get a reaction from the women. She felt she'd made progress in her quest to learn more about them.

"I wouldn't use that word exactly. Malicious is a strong statement," Nanette said. "But, yes, we kept track of what she did in case we had to use it against her."

"We were young," Suzanne replied. "You remember those days. We would never do that now."

"Do you stand by your alibi? You were shopping at a boutique when Amber was murdered."

"Yes." Suzanne bobbed her head once.

"You never left." Serena continued to quiz her. "You stayed in one store for three hours?"

"They serve champagne, Serena." Suzanne tapped her glass. "Plus, it takes time to find the perfect outfit."

"I heard otherwise. A rideshare was involved. I can easily check." Serena watched as the women clutched their drinks. "Care to elaborate?"

"No." Suzanne folded her arms.

"Come on, Suze." Nanette nudged her. "I was starving. The boutique offered nothing to eat, so we asked where we could find a good fast-food burger. Wanting to keep our reputations, we chose not to ask the hotel driver to take us there. The salesperson let us sneak out the back door after she ordered a car for us."

"The boutique never told our investigator you had gone to a restaurant," Serena said.

"To protect us," Nanette replied.

"Tell me the restaurant name, and the time you visited," Serena said in a grim voice. "Although I can guess the burger place. It's In and…"

"Hold on there." Suzanne pointed at her, pressing her lips together. "You didn't want to befriend us girls. You're working for the police."

Impressed by Suzanne's comment, Serena sat up straighter. "No, I don't work for them. Let's say I do my own investigating."

"Nanette leaned on the bar. "You've done this before? Like in your book?"

"Yes and stop changing the subject." Serena dropped her shoulders and said in one long breath. "I don't want you to be guilty because I like you, but my boyfriend, who wants to take it slow, and I want to take things fast, said not to use my emotions when investigating. Use only cold, hard facts." She exhaled, letting out a puff of air. "So give me the facts."

"Taking things fast sometimes doesn't work out," Suzanne grimaced.

"Agree." Nanette directed a thumb toward her sister. "Husband number two."

"Hey, you're doing it again," Serena protested. "We're off topic. Please provide the restaurant name and the time of your arrival and departure." She waved to Alex. "Could I have a pen and paper?"

"Sure thing." Alex bobbed his head. "Give me a minute."

"You can write it down," Serena said. "You don't have to say the fast-food chain aloud if it's against your principles." She fought back a smile.

"Fine." Suzanne took the pen and paper from Alex and scribbled a quick response. "There. You happy?"

"Very." Serena slid from her stool. "And thanks for sharing one of your nicknames. Maybe you didn't notice, Nanette, but you called your sister Suze. What's yours?"

"Nance," Nanette replied. "But you better not tell the others."

"Never." Serena pretended to zip her mouth while she crossed her fingers behind her back with her other hand. *Your friends, no, but Nina and my friends will learn your names.*

"Here you go." Suzanne slid the paper across the bar.

Serena held the paper in the air. "Thanks for the help." She felt like skipping to the elevator. *Should this prove true, I'll remove them from the list.*

"Serena?" a woman's voice called before she reached the elevator.

Serena turned to face her. "Beth?"

"I saw you talking to Suze and Nance. What did they say? They think I did it, don't they?" Beth said in a weepy voice.

Suze and Nance? They really are friends. "No, Beth, they don't." Serena touched Beth's arm. "In their hearts, they thought they were protecting you. They felt if you told your story, you'd have nothing to hide."

"Okay, thanks." Beth sniffed.

"If it makes you feel better," Serena said. "I don't think you did it either."

Chapter Twelve

The elevator doors slid back, and Serena stepped into the hallway which led to the lobby. On the ride down, she remembered her date with Jack, but she hadn't heard from him. Lily also requested her presence at dinner. *Can I do both?*

Serena was so wrapped in her thoughts she didn't notice a man rushing toward her. "Serena?" Justice exclaimed. "There you are."

"Of course, here I am," Serena snapped. "What are you doing here?"

"Checking on you. The girls said they haven't seen you in days."

"An exaggeration of the truth, but, yes, I'm okay." Serena placed her hand on her hip. "The girls are fine. I spoke with them a few hours ago. They never mentioned *you*. I know my daughters, and I'm sure they tried to stop you from coming here to look for me."

Justice hung his head. "I had to see for myself. What mess did you get yourself into this time?"

"*This* time? It's called none of your business."

"Serena." Justice tilted his head. "You only stay overnight at the hotel when something big is going down."

"Are you stalking me, Justice Tate?"

"Would you like me to?" Justice flashed his killer smile.

Serena centered her mind. She thought of Samurai and Nina, her friends waiting for her at the inviting tearoom full of scents and culinary delights. "No, I don't believe you're that kind of man, Justice. Thanks for checking on me. I'm fine, as you can see. I have plans, so I must be going. Have a good evening."

"Aww, baby, you know my concern is real. If you ever need me." Justice pointed at her. "You've got my number."

"Sure." Serena went toward the gardens, taking long strides. The more distance she put between them, the better. *What if Jack saw us? He can't take much more of Justice showing up unannounced.*

When she arrived at the pond, Serena leaned on the railing. "Sam," she whispered.

Sam appeared before she finished saying his name. His expression seemed to say, "What's happening? Did you learn something new?"

"I'm taking Nanette, Suzanne and Beth off the suspect list. I'm finally making progress. Do you agree?" Sam swam in circles and popped up his head. "I'm out of treats. Sorry. I could go to the shop and buy some koi food."

The fish widened his eyes and shook his head. Serena's laugh started to unfold. It began low in her belly and rose up her throat and into her mouth. The sound made her joyful, and she wiped tears from her eyes. "I needed that. You made my day."

"Who made your day?" Jack asked, approaching Serena.

"Sam. My fish. The koi who is…" Serena gazed at the pond. "Gone."

"Serena, I'm glad I found you. Something's come up, and I need to push back our dinner date."

"It's fine, Jack. I'll eat with Mia and Lily. They're in the tearoom waiting for me."

"Two dinner invites. You're a popular girl." Jack teased. "Drinks then?"

Serena checked the time. "It's almost seven. Is nine good?"

"I'll see you there." Jack took her hand. "What did Justice want?"

"Oof!" Serena withheld from stomping her foot. "Nothing gets past you, does it?"

"Not in this hotel."

"Is that why you came looking for me?"

"Partially. I really need to work on something."

"Does it involve Nina?"

"Yes."

"Then work away." Serena snuggled close to him. "Why don't you come to my room instead of meeting at the bar?"

"Some time soon, but not tonight. Besides, Jonathan, your favorite bartender, is working until midnight."

"Then it's a date. I haven't seen him in a while."

Jonathan and Serena had a rocky start to their friendship. After gathering evidence in the model murder case, she thought he might have committed the crime. She hoped he hadn't since they'd bonded over the love of British TV crime shows and reading. Jonathan, with his surfer boy good looks, hadn't appeared the type to be a fan of those two things, but Serena had learned never to judge a book by its cover. A great analogy for an author.

"Enjoy your dinner," Jack said, letting go of her hand. "See you at nine."

* * * *

Surprised to see Nina at the table, Serena rushed to greet her. "I'm so glad you're here. You look wonderful, as always."

Nina waved her hand. "Flattery will get you everywhere. Now, do you have something to report?"

"Yes." Serena took her seat and acknowledged Mia and Lily with a smile. "But I need your help." She told the lengthy tale of Bonnie's visit to her office, ending with the rooftop bar episode.

"Bonnie is Amber's cousin?" Nina placed her hand over her heart. "All these years, I never knew. From what you've told us, Serena, I agree with you. She couldn't have killed her cousin." She met Serena's eyes and grinned. "Although I'd love to learn their nicknames, Suzanne and Nanette will thank you for keeping their secret."

"Are they completely different or do they use part of their names?" Lily asked. "Sorry, I'm curious."

"I'll make you a deal," Serena said. "I wouldn't want you to slip and call them those names, but after everyone leaves, I'll tell you." She held up crossed fingers. "I kind of promised I wouldn't tell."

The women laughed and congratulated Serena on her deceptive move.

Lily lightly clapped her hands. "I love a good mystery. I'm starting a list now. Suzanne could be Susie or Zan."

Serena chuckled as her friend discussed name possibilities. Bright and ambitious, Lily would keep at it until she solved the unknown. "You make the list, and we'll see," she said.

"Let's get back to another list," Mia replied. "The suspect list. You eliminated Bonnie, Nanette, Suzanne and now Beth. Who does it leave?"

Nina ticked off her friends' names. "Diane, Linda, Joan and Sandra. You must focus on them, Serena."

"I never had a one-on-one conversation with Diane. Perhaps I'll start there."

"What about your fish?" Mia asked. "Does he agree with your findings?"

"Mia Takeda Phillips." Serena folded her arms. "Are you doubting Sam is real?" She turned to Nina. "Tell her."

"You must have faith, my dear granddaughter." Nina covered Mia's hand with her own. "You may discover a friend when you least expect it."

"You mean a koi?" Mia wrinkled her nose.

"I cannot say." Nina lifted her chin, and a server arrived in seconds. "We're ready to order, Jun. The kitchen will close soon, and I don't want anyone staying late because of us."

"We don't mind, Mrs. Takeda," Jun answered. "Your presence is always a treat."

Jun took their orders, and Serena looked forward to her dinner of tomato basil soup and chicken salad. The tearoom also served simple grilled chicken and fish dinners, along with roasted vegetables and mashed or sweet potatoes cooked to perfection. Quiche stayed on the menu from breakfast until dinner.

After they'd eaten and ordered another pot of tea, Nina turned towards Serena. "Will you see Jack later?"

"We're meeting after I finish here," Serena answered. "At the bar." She slumped forward. "What can I do to move this relationship to the next level?"

"Jack is not ready," Nina answered. "To you it may appear slow, but for him, it is going at the right pace. We're all different. He wants to get to know you, see if you're compatible. Not like his first wife."

The words caught Serena by surprise. She perked up and leaned forward. "Do tell."

"Not a word to Jack." Nina shook her pointer finger, making eye contact with the three women.

"Nope," Lily said.

"I'll keep it to myself," Mia said. "I won't even tell Kade."

"Same." Serena widened her eyes, waiting to hear the story. "But not the Kade part." She giggled. "Jack never speaks of his ex, except for one story. She convinced him not to get a dragon tattoo. He got the Japanese symbols for the dragon instead. I asked if she preferred the symbols so they could have matching tattoos. Jack said she was afraid of needles and never got one."

"Not fair," Lily replied. "Especially since she didn't want one. She should have let Jack make his own choice."

Serena nodded. "He loved her and wanted to make her happy." She looked at Nina. "Please tell us more about his past life."

"As you know," Nina said. "Jack worked for my husband, Kal, in LA after we separated for a few years."

"A few years?" Mia snorted. "More like ten."

"It is not part of the story, Granddaughter, so it does not matter," Nina huffed. "Jack confided in Kal. My husband shared some details with me. Confidentially, of course. I am only disclosing a part of what I know to help Serena." She took a breath and settled back in her chair. "Jack had met his wife while serving in the armed forces. They dated a short time before he asked her to marry him."

"That's when he got the tattoo," Lily said. "It's common for people to get them while serving."

"Perhaps." Nina rolled her eyes. "Not part of the story, either." She took a sip of tea. "After their tours ended, they came home to LA."

"Both lived in the same area?" Mia asked.

"Yes," Nina answered. "Jack got a job with the LAPD, and his fiancée worked at a local recruiting office. Once they settled into everyday life, they married. Jack worked odd hours, and the fiancée did not."

"Does the fiancée have a name?" Lily questioned.

"Gina. But again…"

"Not part of the story," the three women said in unison.

"Serving in the military and living in LA were two different worlds. Jack and Gina saw each other daily during their tour but less often back home. Jack learned things about her he had not known before. He wanted to start a family. She did not."

"Never?" Serena's heart dropped.

"Let us say she wanted to wait," Nina answered. "Gina was enjoying life."

"Don't tell me," Lily said. "She cheated on our beloved friend."

"I am afraid so." Nina frowned. "After divorcing Gina, Jack quit the police force and now works for Kal. He built a wall around his feelings and has kept up his guard ever since. Serena do not go bulldozing in and try to knock it down in a day. But knowing you." Nina winked. "You will find another way."

"Brick by brick if I must." Serena smiled. "Thanks for sharing something Jack never would."

"Maybe he will one day," Mia said. "This helps you understand him now."

Tears welled in Serena's eyes. "He's like a father-figure to the girls. Now I know why. We could still have a…"

"Serena!" Nina glared at her. "Did you hear me say take it slow?"

* * * *

Serena found Jack sitting at the end of the bar, talking and laughing with Jonathan. The two men played important, yet different, roles in her life, and she was grateful for their presence. She could come to Jonathan when she needed to sort out a character or a plot line when writing her book. Eager to help, he would offer his opinion on what should stay or be changed.

Jack had become her rock, or instead, Serena liked to think of him as a strong oak tree with his roots buried deep in the ground. She could wrap her arms around him, and nothing could dislodge them, no matter how fierce the storm. He made eye contact with her, and her stomach flipped when he gave her a genuine smile. One which said, "I've been waiting for you."

"Hi," Serena slid onto the stool next to Jack. "It appears as if you two were enjoying a joke. Care to let me in?"

"Don't worry, Serena. It wasn't about you." Jonathan teased. "Jack told me about the cheerleaders, and we wished we'd seen it firsthand."

"You were at the station today, Jack. Did Bill Mitchell describe them?" Serena recalled the expression on the man's face when he brought old man Morelli to the memorial. Shock, then humor.

"In detail." Jack shook his head. "To a crowd gathered in his office. He shouldn't have discussed the case, but he loves to be the center of attention."

"You eavesdropped." Serena pointed at Jack with a smirk.

"Okay." Jack held up his hands. "You caught me. I knew the story from you but wanted to hear his version.

You win, Serena. You described the women much better." Jack squeezed her hand and winked. "Drink?"

"In honor of Bill Mitchell, I'll have his drink of choice."

"You heard the woman." Jack laughed. "A Bill Mitchell Special." He turned to Serena. "Which is?"

"Cranberry and soda. If Jonathan didn't make it correctly, Bill requested a new one. I told Jonathan I'd drink the ones Bill returned. I got to like them."

"Did this happen when I banished you to the bar during the last case?" Jack teased.

"Yes, that's how I got to know Jonathan. I spent the entire day at this bar." Serena tapped the wooden surface.

"So, you listened and stayed put."

"I did my best."

Jack ran his hand over his mouth. "I'm not saying a word."

Serena leaned toward him. "You're in a good mood tonight, Jack Ando. I like it. What's the cause?"

"First, you're here, and second, Nina is free."

"I'll drink to both," Serena said, after Jonathan handed her the drink. She tapped Jack's beer bottle with her Bill Mitchell special and kissed his cheek. "To you, my solid oak, and don't ask."

Chapter Thirteen

"Mom, you've got to come home. Jewel and I are having a huge disagreement, and we need you."

"Give me a minute to focus." The call had woken Serena from a deep sleep. *The girls are fighting. Time to go home.* "I'll be there within the hour."

Serena jumped from the bed, threw on jeans and a t-shirt, planning to shower later. She texted the valet as she walked from the bedroom so her car would be ready and waiting. Her handbag sat on a table next to the door, and she easily grabbed it as she sprinted for the elevator.

"What happened?" Tears burned her eyes. "The girls. Jack. The case. None of them are getting my full attention. But how can I do it all? I'm only one person."

The doors slid back when she reached the lobby, and Jack stood in the elevator hallway. She fell into his arms and sobbed, "I'm a terrible mother, Jack. The girls are fighting. I've neglected them. You were right. It's important to spend time with them before they leave for college."

Jack patted her back as Serena took a shuddered breath. "It's okay, Serena. Jade called me. She thought you'd misinterpret her call and asked me to drive you home. She thought you sounded worried and might become distracted on the way home."

"Jade…called…you?" Inside, she lit up with happiness. "You didn't need to…"

"They called. I answered. It's what I do."

"True." Serena placed a hand on his chest. "It's not as bad as I think?"

"Trust me?" Jack's eyes twinkled. "No." He shook his head. "As you say, they're teenagers."

"I love that they called you, Jack," Serena said, handing him her keys. "I'll sit back and relax while you drive." They walked through the lobby and out to her waiting car. "Do you know what they're fighting about?"

"Maybe?" Jack winced. "Let's wait and hear it from them. While I drive, why don't we discuss the case? Did you set up a meeting with Diane Martin?"

"No. I had a busy day."

"Why don't you text her now?"

"Good idea." Serena hesitated. "Although I should stay home today."

"Make a tearoom date for tomorrow. Breakfast."

"Then I'm wasting an entire day."

"Serena." Jack reached for her hand. "The police are no closer to another suspect than you are. I have firsthand knowledge they plan to interview each woman today at the station. You'll probably have to wait until tomorrow to speak with Diane."

"How did you find this out? Certainly not from your nemesis, Bill Mitchell." Serena recalled how Officer Sue Downing had helped Jack with the last case. "Was it Sue?"

"And if it was?" Jack said in a teasing way. "She's my contact at the station. Nothing else."

Jack pulled into Serena's driveway, and she activated the remote to open the door. He continued into the garage and shut down the engine. "I've got work I can do while you speak with the girls. Tiger will pick me up in an hour."

"Tiger? Your boss, the hot guy…"

"Who's married." Jack appeared to fight off a smile. "Yeah, we're going on a day trip. Do some investigating beyond San Francisco."

"Are you going to LA?" Serena asked. "That's where Sandra and Joan live."

"We will start there and may even fly to Naples in the coming days."

"Ooh, so you think it's Diane? I do, too."

"Serena, we're looking into their backgrounds. Nothing more."

"Then you need to visit Columbus, Ohio. That's where Linda lives. I wish I could come."

"I bet you do." Jack winked and opened the car door. "Come on. The girls are waiting."

Serena took a deep breath and exited the car. Her keys jingled in her hand as she unlocked the door leading to the mudroom. "We're home!" she called after Jack entered. "Anyone?"

Robin greeted them in the kitchen doorway. "Serena. Jack. Good to see you both. I told the girls to stay in their bedrooms until you got here. It's a silly argument, but Jade is so serious about it, I suggested she call you."

"You did the right thing, Mama." Serena kissed her cheek, then sniffed. "Have you made breakfast?" She swore she smelled bacon.

"It's almost ready, sweetheart. Jack, would you like a cup of coffee?" Robin asked.

"That sounds wonderful, Robin. Thanks." Jack turned to Serena. "I'll stay in the kitchen with your mom."

"Okay, I'll talk to them upstairs but save some bacon." Serena left the kitchen area and walked up the staircase which led to the girls' bedrooms.

On edge from the chaotic week, she prayed she could handle her girls' problem. Serena stopped at Jewel's door and lightly tapped. "Jewel? It's mom. Will you please come to Jade's bedroom?" She crossed the hall and knocked on another door. "Jade?"

"Come in, Mom."

When Serena entered, she found Jade sitting cross-legged on her bed, reading a book. "I'm sorry I've been away, but I'm here now," she said.

"Mom, do not go there." Jade held up her hand. "This is unrelated to your absence."

Jewel stomped in as if she had the weight of the world on her shoulders. "I told you not to call Mom, Jade. It's stupid."

"Stupid?" Jade unwound her body and threw her legs over the side of the bed.

Serena sat on the edge of the mattress and rested her hand on her daughter's leg before she stood. "Why don't you start from the beginning? Who wants to go first? Jewel? Please sit." She gestured to the dark teal upholstered armchair in the corner.

"Fine." Jewel sat down with a huff and folded her arms over her chest. "We don't need to do everything together, Jade."

"Wait." Serena waved her hand. "Let's start from the beginning, one at a time. Jewel, you can continue stating your case."

"When we're at school, can we do what we want, Mom?" Jewel asked. "Before you say 'within reason', that's exactly what I mean."

"You know me well." Serena chuckled. "Could you give me an example?"

"Classes."

Serena realized they'd never discussed majors or lifelong ambitions or careers. She had gone to community college and transferred to a four-year to finish her degree while she lived at home and dated Justice. Marriage came soon after. *What did I plan to do?* "Have you decided on a major?"

"You don't have to declare yet," Jewel answered. "I want to take exploratory classes to help me decide."

"Such as?"

"Intro to literature or humanities classes. The university grants first-year students some freedom in choosing electives."

"Which is dumb," Jade sneered.

Is this fight about school and class choices? Thank you! Thank you! "It appears Jade disagrees. I'd like to hear from you now." She looked at Jade.

"Mom, Jewel is not thinking about our future."

"It's *my* future, Jade," Jewel yelled.

"See?" Jade pointed at her sister. "She won't listen."

"What I see," Serena said. "Is Jewel wants to make choices independent of yours. That's not so bad."

"She'll regret it." Jade stared at her mom. "We want to become models. We should do whatever it takes to help our careers as soon as possible. Literature is fine, but how will it help us decide if we should get a business or marketing degree?"

I have a dreamer and one who is pragmatic. How do I help them come together? "What course do you want to take?" Serena asked.

"Intro to marketing," Jade answered. "We should learn how to brand ourselves. Understand marketing buzzwords and phrases and their relevance to us now."

"Makes sense."

"We must take the course together, Mom, so Jewel and I can discuss how it can help our careers. Admit it, Jewel, we both want the same thing."

"Yes, we do, but we can follow our own path in college."

"Can you agree to take a few classes together?" Serena asked. "I've got a great idea." She rubbed her hands together. "What if you both take Intro to Marketing and Intro to Literature? Then you can select the rest on your own."

"Maybe," Jewel whispered.

"Jewel," Serena said. "Is that a yes?"

"Okay, yes," Jewel answered. "Only if Jade agrees to take the literature course."

"I will." Jade nodded, appearing as if she had gotten her way. "The best of both worlds."

"Anything else?" Serena asked.

"No." Each girl shook their head.

"Why don't you show me your other choices after breakfast? I'll go over your schedules individually. Remember, I went to college, too."

"Not that again," Jade moaned, then laughed. "I'll come down in a minute."

"Me, too." Jewel hopped from the chair.

"I'm going down now, unless you need me," Serena said. "Jack's here, and he'll be leaving soon."

"Jack is here?" Jade asked. "Why didn't you say so?" She pushed past Serena and rushed out the door with her sister.

Serena stood with her hands on her hips and smiled. "Maybe I can handle it all." She slipped her phone from her pocket and texted Diane. "Let's see when you respond, Mrs. Martin. Or maybe the police have already arrested you."

* * * *

"Mom, did you know Jack is going to LA today?" Jade asked when Serena walked into the kitchen.

"Yes, I did…" Serena stopped mid-sentence. "Are you girls eating breakfast?"

"I have slowly introduced them to some healthy options," Robin answered. "They are having egg white omelets with spinach, onion and pepper."

"You don't even taste the spinach," Jade replied, making a face when she said spinach. "Hot sauce helps, too."

"The ingredients change daily," Jewel said. "Grandma has all kinds of great choices."

And I never did? Whatever. I'm happy they'll eat more than a protein bar. "Do I see bacon on your plate?" Serena squinted and came closer to the island.

"Turkey bacon, Mom." Jade rolled her eyes. "You should try it."

"We're all having turkey bacon today," Jack said. "I like it."

"I guess I'll try it," Serena replied with a dramatic flair. She joined Jack and her mom at the banquette, the cozy table with padded benches placed in the kitchen nook. Surrounded by windows on three sides, it gave a wonderful view of her backyard. Serena met Jack's eyes and asked, "Have you heard from Tiger?"

"He'll be here any minute." Jack finished his coffee and placed the mug on the table. "If I discover anything new or interesting, I'll text you. What about you? Did Diane return your message?"

"Not yet, but it's early." Serena put her phone where she could see it. "Before you leave, can we review what we know about Diane?"

"Why don't you go into the study?" Robin suggested. "It's close to the front door, and you can talk in private."

"Thanks, Mama." Serena took her phone and coffee from the table. "I'll help you clean up after Jack leaves. Don't start without me." She gave her mother a cautionary look.

"Fine." Robin held up her hands. "Can I bear to sit here and look at dirty dishes?"

"You'll manage." Serena smiled.

＊ ＊ ＊ ＊

"First things first," Jack said, taking the coffee and phone from Serena. He put them on a small round table that sat between two armchairs and returned to where she stood. "Come here, beautiful."

"Beautiful?"

"You should hear it more often." Jack pressed his lips together. "I'm adding a little romance to our lives."

"I like it." Serena slid her arms around Jack's neck. "Hello there, handsome."

"Okay, don't get carried away." Jack chuckled.

"Jack." Serena huffed. "You be you, and I'll be me. Deal? No forced romantic words just because you think I want to hear them."

"Nothing's forced, Serena, but I'll try harder to be me."

Serena threw back her head and laughed. "That's my Jack."

"My Jack. I like it."

Jack pulled Serena close to him and lowered his lips onto hers. His gentle kiss grew into a passionate one as the seconds ticked by. Serena longed to kiss him forever, but a buzzing phone put a stop to the tender moment.

Serena stepped back and touched Jack's cheek. "You better get that."

Jack read his message and said, "It's Tiger. He'll be here in five minutes. We better discuss Diane."

Serena walked to the table and checked her phone. "Ooh, Diane replied to my message. She's agreed to meet me for breakfast tomorrow. How should I start the interview?" she asked. "Friendly or business-like."

"Friendly. You invited her to breakfast. Talk about tea choices. Share your favorites on the menu. Warm her up."

"Then go in for the kill."

"That's a little strong." The corner of Jack's mouth twitched.

"Okay, I'll start with her police interview. Ask how it went." Serena paused. "Can I act like I know? It's not a secret, right?"

"Yes, it's alright that you know. Be self-assured when asking questions. You'll do fine. I don't like leaving you again." Jack kissed the tip of her nose. "But duty calls."

"Will you see your parents while in LA?" Serena asked.

"I'll try my best. I hope they've made some progress since I left. Their messages are vague."

"Stay if they need you, Jack. I know the Takeda helicopter is at your disposal."

"We're flying to LA in it." Jack checked his phone. "He's here."

"Where do you land?"

"On top of the Takeda's LA building downtown. We'll grab a company car from the underground parking garage to get to our destination."

"Good luck." Serena reached for his hand, and Jack clasped onto it.

"Same to you." Jack gave a quick squeeze in support and left the room.

Chapter Fourteen

"There are many types of tea," Serena said, pointing to the menu. "Black, green, oolong, rooibos and others, as you see here. You also can choose fruit infused flavors: cherry, blueberry, and peach apricot, my favorite flavor."

"You certainly know a lot about tea," Diane said, perusing the menu. "I think I'll stick with Earl Grey."

"You're missing out then." Serena replied. "Come on, at least try something new. I recommend Angel's Dream, a mix of black and green tea flavored with maple and blackberry. If you don't like it, they'll bring you a pot of Earl Grey."

"You convinced me." Diane touched the menu. "I like the name. Although the week has not been an angel's dream."

"Sorry, Diane. It must be hard." Serena motioned to Jun and gave their order.

"Tea, quiche, and scones, coming right up," Jun said.

Diane let out a breath. "I thought we'd die of old age and never dreamed someone from our group would be murdered in cold blood."

Thanks for opening the door, Diane. "Shocking." Serena leaned back as Jun set teapots in front of her and Diane. "Thanks."

"If you do not care for the tea," Jun said to Diane. "Please feel free to change your order." She turned to Serena. "No oolong today? Trying something new?"

"Jun, I'm not that predictable."

"When it comes to tea you are." Jun teased.

"I thought I'd surprise you." Serena smiled. "Peach apricot is my second favorite."

"I'll remember that." Jun winked as she left the table.

Serena waited until Diane added a spoonful of sugar and took her first sip.

"Mmm. It is good." Diane smiled.

Serena poured her peach apricot tea, stirred in some sugar and said, "The police questioned all of you at the station yesterday. How was that?"

"A long, horrible day. We refused to leave until we could go together. I drank bad coffee and ate cold pizza."

"I hope this makes up for it," Serena said. "How long did it take?"

"Most of the day. I treated the girls to dinner at the restaurant, and Suzanne and Nanette bought drinks at the rooftop bar. Watching the sun set helped." Diane let out a breath.

"Did the police ask about any specific person?"

Diane's brows rose high into her forehead. "Why would they?"

"They're looking for the murderer, right?"

"Look." Diane leaned over the table. "What if no one in our group killed Amber? Huh? What about that? It might be a random person or someone who works at the hotel. Did you or the police look beyond us?" She folded her arms. "That's right. I'm on to you, Serena Tate. You are not our friend. Your primary goal is to help Nina."

"Guilty as charged. I will always defend Nina. My loyalty is to her."

Diane unfolded her arms and reached for her teacup. "Plus, you're gathering information for your next book. I see you writing in your journal."

"I need it with me, Diane. Whenever an idea strikes, I write it down. The current situation has no connection to a book I may write." *Maybe. Okay. Probably.*

Jun served their food, and the conversation stopped. Grateful for the break, Serena plotted her next move. *I've heard her story from other people. I need to hear it firsthand.* "Since we've cleared the air, why don't you tell me your story? I've heard it, but not from you."

"You mean Amber, Stan's and my story, don't you?"

"You could start there." Serena longed for one more scone with clotted cream and lemon curd, yet she resisted.

"I see you staring at those scones," Diane said, moving the plate closer. "Go ahead. We might be here for a while."

"So, you're willing to share," Serena replied, choosing a scone from the plate.

"It's not a secret. I've told the police about my past, and you appear to be fair-minded. I'm aware I have a motive to want Amber dead. but why now?"

"You caught her stealing the pearls, and it brought back memories of your college days." Serena grimaced. "The necklace was in her hand when you killed her." *Sorry, Jack, I went there.*

"What? I did no such thing." Diane's nostrils flared.

"Then tell me this." Serena folded her arms. "How did you learn about the pearls before they became public knowledge?"

"That I can answer." Diane stared at Serena, giving her a look which sent shivers down her spine. "I overheard a police officer asking another if they should look for them."

"When?"

"As they left the hotel that evening. I thought nothing of it until someone told me Amber was dead. And what about those elusive pearls?" Diane pointed at Serena. "Is anyone looking for them? You should focus on that, Serena. Where are they? Once you find them, you have your killer."

I'll check with Jack. I was so busy trying to exonerate Nina, I never thought about the necklace. "You make a valid argument. I'm sure the police are looking for them."

"Are they?" Diane sniffed. "From what I can tell, they want to close the case quickly. Everyone likes Nina, including the police. They're looking for another suspect so they can completely exonerate her."

"What if I promise to investigate the pearls' disappearance? Whoever possesses them can't sell to a pawnshop or a buyer. The police are watching and probably have sent out an alert nationwide. I believe the person who stole the necklace still has them in their possession."

"They probably don't know what to do with them," Diane stated. "I would have them taken apart and made into other pieces."

"Would you?" Serena lifted a brow. *She has the means to do so.*

"But why would I? I could buy my own."

"Jealousy? Nina's dad gifted her a string of pearls."

"That was long ago. If I wanted pearls, I could have asked my dad to buy me a necklace."

"Nina didn't ask. Her father presented her with the pearls on her twenty-first birthday."

"Whatever. I could have mentioned I loved her pearls and gotten a necklace for my birthday," Diane replied. "I don't want to argue over jewelry, Serena. Promise me you'll start searching today."

"I promise," Serena said. "Now I'd like to hear your story."

Diane's account matched what the others had told Serena. She hadn't liked Amber from the start or the fact that Amber's father bought her way onto the team. Diane admitted she had held a grudge against Beth for her betrayal but finally let it go. In the end, Diane married Stan, which she felt was payback enough for Amber.

"Was it payback?" Serena asked. "Amber's love of her life changed throughout college. By junior year, Sandra's husband became her target."

Serena doubted Diane was telling the entire truth. Stan was not on Amber's radar for long. She had moved on to another and never looked at Stan again. Diane must have eventually realized it, too. Marrying Stan didn't make them even.

"Does it matter?" Diane asked. "Amber got what she deserved. A sad, lonely life."

A twinge of sympathy stirred in Serena. After meeting Mr. Morelli, she felt Amber never stood a chance. She only wanted his love and acceptance, so she acted accordingly. "Let's move on," she said. "To the wedding."

"Which one?" Diane asked with a laugh.

"Joan invited the team to her daughter's wedding," Serena answered. "She hoped everyone would reconnect after all those years apart. Is that when you brought up the idea of five-year reunions?"

"Yes." Diane nodded. "Look how it turned out. I got one of the team killed."

Either Diane was a good actress or she was telling the truth. Serena didn't know which one to believe. Diane had answered all her questions and seemed eager to discover who had killed Amber, but Serena viewed her as a hostile witness. The longer they spoke, the icier her tone. *I thought you did it, Diane. Now I'm not so sure. Time to call a P.I.C. meeting.*

"I'll be right back," Diane said, gesturing to the ladies' room.

"Perfect time to send a message," Serena whispered after Diane had left the table. She asked Lily and Mia to come to the tearoom when their schedules allowed. *Not an emergency*, she added before sending.

When Diane returned, she stood by the table. "Thanks for breakfast, Serena. It's getting late, and I have things to do. I've tried to reason with you and answer your questions, but to no avail. Don't contact me again. We're done here."

Serena found herself at a loss for words. Diane called her out and had every right to do so. Yet it didn't stop Serena from suspecting her of murder. "Sure. I understand," she finally said.

Pouring another cup of tea, Serna inhaled the peach apricot scent. She planned to wait until Mia and Lily arrived and debated if she should order more tea.

"Quite the interesting story," Nina said, surprising Serena with her appearance.

"My gosh, Nina, where did you come from?" Serena rested her hand on her heart. "Is there a secret room we don't know about?"

"Oh, no, my child." Nina chuckled. "Just excellent hearing."

"Please join me."

"I can only stay a minute." Nina slid into the chair she always sat in. "You think Diane killed Amber, don't you?"

"Yes." Serena hung her head. "After what she said today, I'm having doubts."

"I agree with one thing she said. We need to find the pearls. How do we go about it?"

"That's the million-dollar question. I'm stumped." Serena wrapped her hands around her teacup. "I'll call Jack later to see if the police are searching for the necklace. After that?" Serena shrugged.

"I'll let you be. Give you time to think." Nina rose from her chair. "I still run a hotel you know." She winked.

"Before you go, let me ask you a question," Serena said, stirring her tea. "Who do *you* think killed Amber?" She glanced up, only to find Nina had left without a sound. "Darn. How does she do that?"

"Serena," Mia said, placing her hand on Serena's shoulder. "I saw Grandmother as I came in. She said I'd find you at our table."

"You saw her? I thought she vanished in a puff of smoke." Serena smiled.

"Grandmother is excellent at making a mysterious exit," Mia said. "I see you ordered tea."

"It's from my breakfast date with Diane. I intended to place an order for you and Lily, but Nina stopped by."

"In a puff of smoke?" Mia giggled.

"Something like that. She heard my entire conversation with Diane."

"Wow. She has superpowers." Mia gestured toward the entrance. "Lily's here. On my way in, I saw Jun and requested tea. I hope Lily doesn't do the same thing." She lifted her hand. "Lily?"

"Hello," Lily said, sitting in her usual seat. "You realize it's almost lunchtime? I might order some cucumber sandwiches."

"Coming right up," Jun said, putting teapots in front of Lily and Mia. "Anything else?"

"Not right now, Jun, thanks," Mia answered. She turned to Serena. "Did you learn anything new?"

"Diane seems determined to discover who killed Amber. Does that sound like a guilty person?"

"No, but is she trying to mislead you?" Lily asked. "Diane is smart. She must know you suspect her."

"That's why she is still on my list," Serena answered. "Diane also brought up an excellent point. Who is looking for the necklace?"

"The police?" Mia wrinkled her nose. "At least they should be."

"I should call Jack."

"But he's in LA with Tiger working on the case," Lily said and raised her shoulder. "I work downstairs. I know things." She smiled at Serena. "And you don't want to bother him."

"Bother him, Serena," Mia replied. "Tell him you have a quick question."

"Okay." Serena opened her phone and called him.

"Serena, are you alright? I just saw you a few hours ago, I hope nothing's happened," Jack said in a rush after answering her call.

"I'm fine, Jack. We have a question."

"We?"

"I'm at the tearoom with Lily and Mia."

"Talking about the case."

"Yes. We wondered if the police are searching for the necklace."

"They have sent out notices to local shops and dealers, plus to other police stations in the area. Probably nationwide, too."

"Are the police actively searching for it? Have they assigned someone to find the pearls?"

"Good question. I'll get back to you on that."

"One more thing, Jack. After speaking with Diane, I have a few theories. The killer still has the necklace or has hidden it somewhere. Find the necklace, and it will lead to the murderer. If I wanted to investigate, where should I start?"

"At the crime scene and work your way from there," Jack answered. "Put yourself in the suspect's shoes. What would you do?"

"Thanks, Jack. You've helped a lot. Any luck in LA?"

"Not yet, but I'll text if we find something. See you tonight…hopefully."

"Great. See you then." Serena ended the call and looked at her friends. "If you stole the pearls, what would you do with them?"

"I would sell them," Lily answered. "Then I'd realize what a colossal mistake that was. Everyone is looking for the necklace, so I couldn't visit a local pawnshop or dealer. I'd wait until I got home, and things cooled down."

"So the killer still has the pearls in their possession," Mia said, holding up her pointer finger. "Could security search their rooms?"

"Not without cause," Serena answered.

"There is cause," Mia replied.

"This is a police matter, Mia. Pearl's security can't bust into rooms and search through people's personal effects."

"Who would be stupid enough to hide the pearls in their room?" Lily questioned. "They might get a deposit box at a bank for safekeeping." She tapped her chin. "I'll get on that. Or…"

"Put the necklace in someone else's room. Set them up. This person may have arrived at the same conclusion as us. It's too dangerous to sell the pearls or keep them in her hotel room," Serena said. She tapped the table. "The police need to get warrants to search everyone's rooms immediately. Too bad Jack left the force. He'd do it."

"Um." Lily bit into her bottom lip. "We should stop talking. Trouble is coming our way."

Eight women surrounded the table. Each with a hand on her hip.

"We've had enough of your accusations, Serena," Diane said. "We're here as a group to tell you to leave us alone."

"I'm sorry you feel that way." Serena made eye contact with Bonnie, then Suzanne and Nanette. They didn't seem angry or upset. "Perhaps it's just some of you."

"Regardless," Diane continued. "You heard our request." She turned on her heel. "Come on, girls."

"Sorry," Nanette mouthed, but followed behind the others.

"Well, I guess she told me." Serena rolled her eyes. "I don't need them anymore. Let's contact Nina and tell her we plan to focus on the necklace. I want to examine her apartment with fresh eyes."

"You don't need to call, Serena," Nina said. The three women jumped at the sight of her. "Why are you so skittish?" she asked.

"Where did you come from?" Mia asked her grandmother.

"I was behind the girls. You must not have seen me." Nina turned to Serena. "You've thought of something. The look on your face tells me everything."

"Would you take us to your apartment, Nina? I want to start there."

"Certainly." Nina walked toward the exit, and the three women hurriedly pushed back their chairs to join her.

Chapter Fifteen

Once they arrived at Nina's apartment, Serena announced, "I'd like to reenact the crime. I'll play the part of the killer."

"Ooh, I'll be the victim," Lily volunteered.

"Okay. Would you mind standing outside the door?" Serena asked while Nina let them into her luxurious penthouse apartment.

"Sure." Lily saluted.

"You're Amber, and call me Diane," Serena told her.

After Nina closed the door, Serena said, "Okay. This is how I picture it. Diane has the pearls in her hand, ready to leave."

"We don't know if Diane did it," Mia said.

"It's easier to use a name so I chose my number one suspect," Serena answered. "Now where was I?" She paused. "The perpetrator thinks they got away with the crime until they are ready to exit. But! What do they find?" Serena opens the door, revealing Lily on the other side.

"Serena…oh, I mean Diane… what are you doing? Are those Nina's pearls?" Lily asked, relishing her role as Amber. She pointed to Serena's hand and gasped.

"Shocked to see Amber, Diane walks back into the apartment." Serena turned and motioned for everyone to follow her. "They argue. Amber threatens to tell Nina or call the police. She heads for the door, and Diane searches for something to stop her. She spots the knife set in the kitchen and pulls one from its container. Amber is now in the hallway, and Diane pursues her, thrusting the knife into her back."

"Diane is smart enough to clean her fingerprints from the knife and inside the apartment," Lily said. "But clever enough to realize she had visited the night before with the others."

"That makes sense." Mia replied. "Diane needs to leave some evidence she was here."

"Exactly. Diane doesn't need to make a clean sweep of the apartment and lose precious minutes," Serena answered. "With pearls in hand, she heads to the elevator, intending to stash the necklace in her room until she finds a more secure hiding place."

"I have another premise," Nina said. "The girls are all on one floor. Perhaps someone intervened before she got to her room."

"That would totally change things." Mia nodded at her grandmother. "After what happened, all her carefully laid plans have just fallen apart. Someone may have seen her or engaged her in conversation after she stepped off the elevator. The encounter gives her the idea of hiding the necklace in someone's room, with or without their knowledge. Diane is smart enough to realize once the police find the pearls, they'll have their killer."

"All that's left is to frame another woman," Serena said, smiling at her friends. "We make a great team."

"Although this is pure speculation, let's go into my apartment," Nina offered. "My nephews, Kaito and Ken, are the only residents on the floor, but I'd like to keep this between us."

After Serena took her seat in the living room, her phone rang. Seeing Jack's name on the screen, she hopped up and walked into the kitchen to answer. "Jack?"

"Hi, where are you right now?"

"Nina's apartment."

"With Nina?"

"Yes, Mia and Lily are here, too."

"Ask if they can stay a few hours. I want you all in one place."

"Did you discover something?"

"Yes, and no. I'll tell you more when I see you."

"We did a reenactment of the crime, Jack, like you suggested."

"I don't recall saying to act it out, but okay."

"It helped," Serena said in an excited voice. "We think the suspect may have the necklace in their room or put it in someone else's to frame them. What's the latest on the search warrants?"

"I spoke with Sue at the station and suggested the police get warrants to inspect the women's rooms. She agreed, but Bill still calls the shots. We're betting he doesn't want to upset them because they're Nina's friends."

Serena loudly exhaled. "I can't believe Bill backed off and won't do his job. Is August Morelli connected to this? I learned Bonnie Urban is his niece. August may have told Bill to leave Bonnie alone."

"Could be a factor."

"Besides, these women are not Nina's friends, Jack, and you know it. Tell them to search away."

"I'll try my best, but as you are aware, I'm not on the force anymore. Tiger and I are heading for the station after we land. We're on our way home now. Hopefully, Sue talks some sense into Bill before we arrive."

"Did you pass along our theories?"

"Sue concurs that they must search the women's rooms. She may consult the sergeant if Bill fails to file an affidavit for the warrants."

"Sergeant?"

"The head of the department. She's a reasonable woman."

"Good. I hope Sue stays true to her convictions." Serena paused. "We'll wait here until you contact me again. Good luck." She ended the call and returned to the living room. "Jack's pushing Sue to get the warrants. He asked if we'd stay together until he contacts me again."

"Did he give a reason?" Nina asked.

"No," Serena answered. "But I think it's for his peace of mind."

"Kade and Gabe are in LA, so we're free, right Mia?" Lily said.

"What about you, Serena?" Mia asked.

"I'm good. I told Mama I'd stay at the hotel until tomorrow."

"Then we agree. We remain here for a few hours." Nina stood and went to her kitchen. "I have iced tea, water or soda. Ladies?"

"I'll help," Serena said, hopping from her seat. "I'm too nervous to stay in one place."

* * * *

"Jack!" Since no one else had access to the floor, Serena offered to answer Nina's door. She longed to throw her arms around him but refrained, especially after Nina had disclosed his marital history.

"Good. You're all here." Jack seemed eager to share his findings. "The police should arrive within the hour with warrants to search the rooms. Nina, you'll go to the lobby to greet and escort them to the proper floor. While we wait, I'll share what we learned in LA."

"Can I pour you something to drink?" Nina asked.

"Water is fine." Jack sat next to Serena on the sofa. "We discovered one woman is withholding information from the others," he said.

"Who?" Nina appeared surprised.

"Joan."

"Did she file for bankruptcy?" Lily asked.

"Was she arrested for stealing or shoplifting?" Serena winced.

Jack grimaced. "It's a little more personal. Her husband asked for a divorce."

"Oh, no, poor thing." Nina placed her hand on her cheek. "What does her divorce have to do with the murder?"

"Maybe nothing, but it's motive for stealing the necklace. Her husband had filed the divorce papers, so I could read them. It's a fair settlement, but Joan won't live the life of luxury she's accustomed to. She never worked, and the husband is giving her a monthly stipend. Joan couldn't afford to run the house on the amount, so they're selling it. He expects her to use that money for anything she needs to begin her new life. No child support, of course. Their child is an adult."

"She stole the pearls!" Mia exclaimed. "It makes sense. No one would suspect her. She takes them home for safekeeping and sells them later."

"Joan married a high-powered divorce attorney," Jack said. "He was fair but not generous and worded the document so it would hold up in court if Joan contested it."

"All the more reason to steal the pearls. Joan needed money. She never meant to kill Amber. *That* poor woman was in the wrong place at the right time." Serena closed her eyes and pictured her board. *Four left. Diane, Linda, Joan and Sandra.* "Let's focus on Diane and Joan," she said. "I'm ruling out Sandra."

"What about Linda? Is she still on your board?" Jack asked.

"She stays," Serena answered.

Jack checked his watch. "Nina, it's time. Please head down to the lobby. I'll bring Mia, Lily and Serena to the women's floor at the appropriate time."

"When the police arrive, I'll send you a message," Nina said, rising from her chair. "Where is Tiger?"

"He's waiting for you in the lobby. Don't worry, Nina, you won't be alone."

Serena's heart pounded as she watched a composed Nina walk to the door. A sudden urge to see Samurai swept over her. *I'll speak with him later. He'll see the police enter the hotel and possibly hear something. Wait! Why do I think a fish can help me? Because he can.*

* * * *

"I wish your phone would ring," Serena exclaimed. "The minutes seem like hours. It's pure torture waiting."

"Serena," Jack answered. "I feel the same way, but don't worry. She'll call."

"You feel the same? You don't act like it. I've been pacing the halls and biting my nails." Serena examined her hand. "Not literally biting. I'd ruin this great manicure."

"I'm curious to see if our theory is correct." Lily said. "Did Diane frame someone or are the pearls still in her room?"

"I'd like to know that answer, too," Mia replied. "Perhaps we should stop pointing the finger at Diane and refer to the person as the suspect or perpetrator. Our reenactment is over."

"True." Lily nodded. "From now on, it's the suspect, not Diane."

"Jack," Serena said. "We've manufactured this entire scenario and won't know if we're right until the police search the rooms. The suspect could have hidden the necklace in another woman's room or still has it. We don't know for sure."

"The suspect is smart," Lily said. "I believe she visited one of the women and hid the pearls in their room. Now this person is at risk. She can identify the killer."

"It's possible, but the innocent party could also be clueless," Jack said. "We'll get our answers soon."

"Could these women turn on each other?" Serena asked. "To save themselves?"

"From the stories we've heard?" Mia wrinkled her nose. "I think so."

"Text came in." Jack held up his phone. "The police have arrived. We need to give them time to search the rooms."

"It might take a while to go through eight suites," Lily commented. "What about Pearl security, Jack? Have they examined the footage from that floor?'

"Yes." Jack hung his head. "Unfortunately, there is a glitch in the video."

"What?" Lily's jaw dropped. "Someone erased Nina's footage, and now the women's floor has a glitch. What does this tell you?"

"Our suspect is tech savvy?" Serena replied. "Jack, could one of those women break into the security offices and tamper with the equipment?"

"Easily? No. We'd know if someone entered illegally," Jack answered. He covered his mouth and stared at the ceiling. "The only method to gain access to the area without setting off an alarm requires a security tag." Jack paused. "I need to go to the office, but can you please stay here?" He rose from his seat. "I'll come for you when the time is right."

"Jack?" Serena put her hand in his. "You've thought of something."

"Actually, two things. First, I want to connect with Sue. She's a member of the detective squad, and her background in nursing led Sue to forensics. She'll be with the team. I'll tell her wherever they find the necklace, the person may be the victim, not the killer. Until they are certain, the police must keep this individual safe."

Serena widened her eyes. "Warn her that the suspect may silence this woman for good if they don't protect her."

"*If* she is a victim." Jack raised his shoulder. "But I would rather be proactive than discover too late you were right."

"And second?"

"After speaking with Sue, I'll head to the basement and inform The Pearl's team to do a more thorough search. They must review the security footage, checking every person who entered and exited the day of the murder."

"Then go." Serena squeezed his hand. "Don't worry about us. We'll wait here."

After Jack left the apartment, the three women sat in silence. Serena looked at her friends, seeing the sadness and confusion on their faces. Finally, she said, "After this is over, we need to give Nina our full support. When she told us about her sorority reunion, we found it humorous instead of seeing it as a significant part of Nina's past. Let's remember these women have lived for over seventy years, including all the baggage that comes with it."

"Quite profound, Serena," Lily said. "Nina never spoke about her college years, and now she's being forced to relive them, whether she likes it or not. We need to acknowledge her cheerleading past and encourage her to share her feelings. Hearing the women's stories, I understand why Nina chose to leave that part of her life behind."

"We don't see her as weak or needing us," Mia whispered. "Everyone looks to Grandmother for guidance and to solve problems, never checking to see how she feels. I swear I'll do better."

"Amen to that," Serena said. Her phone pinged. "It's Jack. He's coming to get us."

"Let's clean up this mess." Lily pointed to the tray of drinks and glasses on different tables. "But first." She extended her hands to Mia and Serena. "Know this. I'll always have your backs. You can count on me."

Serena grasped onto Lily's hand and reached for Mia's. "I feel the same way."

"I'm here for you, too," Mia said as a tear escaped her eye. "Let's finish this for Grandmother. Hopefully she'll get her beloved necklace returned."

The lump in Serena's throat had grown, and she could only nod. *In one piece, I hope.*

* * * *

"Bill will not like that we showed up," Jack said. "We might not see him, but if we do, try to ignore him."

"Too bad if he sees us," Serena replied. "You are part of Nina's security force, and we must protect her."

"We? So, now you're part of the force?" Jack chuckled.

Serena nudged him with her elbow and bit back a smile.

"And I'm her granddaughter," Mia added.

"If you don't mind, I feel like I'm needed elsewhere," Lily said. "I want to dive into the security footage again. Dig deeper."

"We won't stop you," Mia said. "You appear eager to resume your work."

Jack held open Nina's apartment door. "Shall we?"

The elevator stopped at the women's floor, and Mia, Serena and Jack exited the cubicle. Serena gave a wave to Lily as the doors slid shut. Farther down the hall, Nina spoke with an officer who resembled Sue.

When Nina noticed the trio, she pointed their way. With a serious expression, the officer faced them. "I had no idea the women would be this difficult, Jack," she said. "Why didn't you warn me? They're together in one room with an officer to maintain the peace while we examine the remaining suites."

I was right. It is Sue. Serena stayed silent, letting Jack take charge.

"Who is the most vocal?" Jack asked.

"Diane Martin. She appears to be the leader of the group. The sisters, along with Bonnie, were the most cooperative. We've finished searching their rooms and found nothing."

"Sue, I won't keep you any longer," Nina said. "Please find my pearls."

"I'll do my best, Mrs. Takeda. Joan Field's room is next on my list." Sue held up a key card. "I'll get started."

"Sue," Jack called to her. "Remember our talk."

"I intend to speak to him, but Bill *will* bring the suspect in for questioning, regardless of what we say. I'll drop the 'we need to protect her' once we're back at headquarters."

Sue unlocked a door farther down the hallway, and Serena assumed the room belonged to Joan. "She's the only one going in, Jack. Perhaps the officers are busy elsewhere?"

"Bill probably assigned rooms to his team. Someone will join Sue soon."

"Can we sneak in, Jack? Look around?" Serena pleaded.

"No, but let me check."

"So that's a yes?"

"Follow me." Jack used his security key to unlock Joan's door. "Sue? It's Jack. Is it okay if we come in?"

"You've got ten minutes, Jack," Sue said, appearing in the hallway. "My partner is helping in another suite." She held up her cellphone. "Just received a text from him."

"We'll stay out here," Jack said.

Sue nodded and returned to the bedroom. Besides the bathroom, the suite had two rooms, like Serena's. Familiar with the furniture and décor, she scanned the room, pretending she was the killer. "If I wanted to hide something quickly, I'd choose this room, Jack."

"Okay, where?"

"Someplace Joan wouldn't use, like a drawer." Serena sat on the arm of the sofa to study the room. "That's it!" She hopped up and grabbed Jack's arm. "If all suites are identical, this is a sofa bed. Help me open it."

"Wait. If the pearls are here, Sue must locate them, not us."

"Did I hear my name?" Sue asked, rushing from the other room. "What did you find?"

"Nothing yet, but we have an idea." Jack had already moved the coffee table, and Serena piled the sofa cushions on the floor. "Help us open the sofa bed," he said.

As the trio lowered the mattress to the floor, Nina's pearls slid down the silky material and landed in the middle of the bed. Serena gasped and held back a victory yell. "Nina's pearls," she whispered.

Serena made eye contact with Jack. "Let's leave so Sue can do her job."

Chapter Sixteen

"I didn't do it!" Joan yelled as two officers escorted her down the hallway. When she passed by Serena. she made eye contact. "Help me, please."

"Now you want my assistance?" Although she planned to help exonerate the person who had the pearls, Serena acted like the wounded party. *I believe you were set up, Joan, but the station is the best place for you.*

"Please, I beg you."

"I'll come to the station," Serena said. "We'll talk there."

"Thank you," Joan cried as she entered the elevator.

"This is awful," Sandra said, tugging on Serena's arm. "She is going through a tough time. Will you really go to see her?"

"I always keep my word, Sandra." Serena faced her. "You said it's a tough time for Joan. Like going through a divorce?"

Sandra widened her eyes. "How did you know?"

"We have great intel at The Pearl. Some may think Joan stole those pearls because she needed money."

"Joan would never do that," Sandra snapped.

"The police may think she's guilty after finding the pearls in her room," Serena answered. "Look, if it makes you feel better, I don't think Joan stole the necklace or killed Amber. I'm stating the facts, which is how the police will see it."

"I understand." Sandra said in a kinder voice, "Anything I can do to help?"

"Where was Joan when the murder happened?"

"In her room."

"By herself?"

"Yes, we had dinner and planned to rest before the Goodbye ceremony."

Serena bit her bottom lip, knowing she must remain serious. "Is this a reunion tradition?" she asked.

"Diane insists." Sandra nodded. "We choose the next reunion date and who will host the weekend. This time, Nina got the honors. We open a bottle of champagne and give a toast to the hostess. Then, she passes the torch, an unopened champagne bottle, to the new person in charge. Usually, we open more than one bottle and continue the party."

Sounds like the closing ceremony of the Olympics. Serena refrained from rolling her eyes. "After all that's happened, are you still planning to meet?"

"Yes, once the police solve this case," Sandra answered. "We haven't chosen a day or time since the police ordered us to stay at the hotel. When it happens, I highly doubt it will be celebratory."

"I'd vote to disband the team and cancel all further reunions," Serena said. "Just saying."

"We probably will." Sandra's voice held a touch of sadness. "How can we come together when someone murdered one of our team members?" She seemed perplexed.

"Especially if someone in the group killed Amber."

"Diane doesn't think so. She feels we need to stage a protest. Insist the police look elsewhere."

"The police follow the evidence and facts, Sandra. You can't make them do anything unless you have concrete proof. Do you?"

"Maybe."

What? Sandra is holding back evidence or knows something. "Care to share?" Serena lifted her brows.

"Since everyone is in the hallway, let's wait until things quiet down. Come to my room after you speak with Joan."

"Is Joan aware of this evidence?" Serena stared at Sandra, hoping to make her squirm.

"Yes. We found it together."

"Obviously, you didn't stash it in your room. The police would have found it."

"Correct." Sandra looked over her shoulder. "The girls want to unwind after this horrible disruption of our day. We're going to the sushi restaurant. Text me when you're on your way back from the station."

Sushi? Serena realized she hadn't eaten since late morning. "First, I'm having dinner with my boyfriend," she said. *Boyfriend? Did I just say that?*

Serena spotted Jack almost at the elevator. She hurried to catch up with him and slipped her arm through his. "You're taking me to dinner," she whispered. "How does sushi sound?"

* * * *

"Who looks the guiltiest?" Serena asked, using her chopsticks to add a spicy tuna roll to her plate.

Jack had checked the seating chart upon arrival. He then requested a back corner table where he and Serena could view the seven women without looking suspicious.

"They all do." Jack chuckled.

"We can't stare at them too much," Serena said. "I told Sandra I had a date."

"Should I kiss you?" Jack teased.

"Yes." Serena popped the roll into her mouth.

Jack laughed, and Serena enjoyed hearing the wonderful, genuine sound. "My turn." He chose a salmon topped roll with onion and mayo.

"Now you're playing dirty," Serena said. "I will reject the kiss."

"Oh, I forgot. You don't like onions," Jack replied, half chuckling.

"You didn't forget, Jack." Serena pretended to be annoyed. "You just don't want to kiss me."

Their playful banter went on throughout dinner, while they kept a side eye on the table of seven. "Diane is taking over the conversation," Jack said, giving Serena a wink.

"We must look as if we are on a date and not watching them. Let's pretend I said something funny."

Serena giggled, and Jack took her hand and kissed it.

"I'm not surprised Diane is the only one talking," Serena replied. "What about the rest of them?"

"Suzanne, Nanette and Bonnie seem the calmest. I hope they're not acting. We want to believe they are innocent."

"Anyone acting strange or nervous?"

"Not really. Sandra keeps looking over here," Jack said. "She's checking to see if you're still here."

"I'm ready to leave, Jack, but I am having too much fun."

"We needed this, Serena. What's the saying? All work and no play make Jack a dull boy."

"Never." Serena huffed. "But you're right. Let's promise to do this more often."

"I promise."

"I'm staying overnight, Jack, so I'll return to the hotel after speaking with Joan. Can we meet for a drink or coffee?"

"No." Jack shook his head.

Serena's heart dropped to her stomach. "That's fine." She pushed back her chair, blinking to catch the tears.

Jack placed his hand on her arm. "I said no because I'm coming with you. You won't need to report back to me. We'll interview Joan together."

Delighted by the turn of events, Serena grasped Jack's hand. "Great idea. Let's make a grand exit."

Jack slipped his arm around Serena's waist and walked to the women's table. He lowered his head and said, "Have a pleasant evening, ladies."

* * * *

When Jack and Serena arrived at the station, they checked in at the window and sat in the waiting area. After a few minutes, an officer called to them and led the couple into a small room. While they waited for Joan, Jack announced, "After this interview, I'm leaving for Naples."

"Tonight?"

"Yes. Tiger and I didn't finish the investigation. The plan is to land in Naples tonight and start the search for clues that may help us."

"Diane won't like it. She'll learn you went to her hometown."

"Too bad. If she has nothing to hide, she has nothing to worry about. From there, we'll head to Linda's hometown in Ohio."

"Columbus, right?" Serena asked.

"Yes." Jack nodded. "It's the last stop. No matter what we find, we'll fly home from there."

The door opened, and an officer escorted Joan into the room. He gestured to the chair across from Serena and Jack. "Sit there."

No handcuffs. Good. Maybe Bill got the memo. "Hello, Joan," Serena said.

"What is he doing here?" Joan cocked her head toward Jack.

"He's on your side, Joan," Serena answered.

"My side?"

"Yes," Jack replied. "I've strongly suggested the police keep you here for your own safety."

"That makes no sense." Joan leaned back and blew through her lips.

"Listen, Joan." Serena placed her hands on the table. "Someone in your group killed Amber. What would prevent them from doing the same to you? You had a conversation with that person right after the murder happened. You may have invited them into your room giving them the chance to plant the necklace."

"I did all that?" Joan wrinkled her brow. "That's a lot of assuming."

"Okay, then you tell us."

"I saw no one during that time. After dinner, we returned to our rooms. Sandra and I planned to take a break before going out again. We also wanted to change clothes before heading up to the rooftop bar."

That checks out. "You stayed in your room until then," Serena stated.

"It's hard to remember every moment of that day. Give me a minute to think," Joan said. She glanced at the ceiling. "This might be nothing, but I remember a knock at my door. When I answered, no one was there. I thought it might be Sandra, so I walked down the hall to ask her in person."

"Did you go into her room?" Jack asked.

"Yes, we spoke for a few minutes and joked about how I was hearing things. I decided I imagined it."

Serena faced Jack. "Enough time for the killer to enter her room with no one seeing her." She looked at Joan. "You saw no one."

"Hall was empty."

"Sorry, but that's not helpful." Serena sighed, slumping in her chair. "We assumed you had invited the killer in, and she stashed the necklace when you were distracted. We were counting on you to identify her, but it seems we've come to another dead end."

"Not really. Did Sandra tell you about our discovery?"

"Yes," Serena said. "But she never said what it was."

"It might prove someone else did it and exonerate the girls. Then it won't matter if I saw anyone in the hallway or not."

"Stop being so cryptic. Just tell me." Frustration filled Serena's voice.

"I can't. We made a promise to only use what we found if necessary. Have Sandra show you," Joan said. "Maybe it's nothing, like the knock on the door."

"Serena, we should go." Jack offered his hand. "Joan, I hope you understand why you will stay at the station. Safety first."

Joan ran her hand through her hair and shook her head. "I'm tired and want this to end."

"We're trying our best," Serena said, taking Jack's hand as he knocked to be let out. "Hang in there, Joan." She tried to give her a smile but failed.

"Wait. I thought of something." Joan held up her pointer finger. "When I went to Sandra's room, I used the security latch to keep the door from locking."

"Now *that* is helpful," Serena said. "I've done it before, too. Anyone could have entered your room. Thanks, Joan."

Once outside the station, Serena inhaled the fresh night air. "I can picture what happened, Jack."

"I bet you can." Jack chuckled.

"Diane hid in her room after she knocked on Joan's door. She probably did a happy dance when Joan went down the hall, then a backflip when she discovered the door propped open."

"Wow, you paint a vivid picture."

"It was so easy. Diane couldn't believe her good fortune. She plants the necklace and is back in her room before anyone sees her." Serena slid into the passenger seat of Jack's car. "Makes sense." She checked to see if he agreed.

"It does." Jack leaned toward her. "You're becoming a great detective."

Serena followed his lead and kissed him gently. "I don't want you to leave but please find something."

"I feel the same way," Jack said. "Tiger and I are leaving as soon as we get back to the hotel."

As they drove, Serena gazed out the window, attempting to align all the scattered pieces in her mind. When they reached the hotel, Jack pulled up to the front entrance and dropped her off. Tiger hurried from the building, acknowledging Serena with a brief nod before joining Jack in the car. She remained on the sidewalk and watched the SUV until it vanished into the flow of traffic. "Good luck," she whispered.

The hotel's automatic doors slid back, and Serena stepped into her favorite home-away-from home. She soaked in her surroundings, then heard a woman's voice call her.

"Serena, over here." Lily stood by the red Torii gate as if she'd been waiting for her.

"Lily, it's good to see a friendly face."

Lily hugged her. "Let's walk." She tilted her head toward the gardens. "I repaired part of the security tape. Enough to see a blonde woman enter Joan's room."

"Joan doesn't have blonde hair," Serena exclaimed. "Which brings my list down to two suspects."

"Diane and Linda," they said in unison.

When they reached the pond, Serena headed for the bench. Samurai would not appear until Lily left, but she could wait. "Joan insists Sandra has evidence that would clear all the girls." Serena pursed her lips. "She called them girls, not me."

"What I found trumps her claim," Lily said. "But no harm checking it out." She let out a breath. "It's getting late. Sandra might be asleep."

"True. I'll ask if Mia, you, and I can meet her in the morning. We all need to be there." Serena dashed off a text.

"Let's see if she answers," Lily said. "I'll stay for a few more minutes. Gabe and Kade are due back any minute. I want to greet him."

"Go." Serena nudged Lily. "I'll send you the details."

"You sure?" Lily rose from the bench.

"Positive." Serena breathed in the floral scents from the garden and relaxed on the bench. She needed a moment to herself. Only a few people strolled the area late at night, giving Serena the peaceful time she needed. The only sound was the fountain spraying water into the pond. Finally, she leaned forward to check the time and said under her breath, "It's almost midnight. I hope you're not asleep, Sam."

A red head emerged from the water. "Well, aren't you the night owl?" She chuckled and walked to the fence. "I assume you heard everything."

Samurai swam in a circle and lifted his head from the water. He looked so eager to help, it melted her heart. "If only you could talk. Okay, here it goes. Yes or no questions. Should I check out Sandra's evidence?"

After a deep dive, the fish sprang from the water.

"That's a yes. Do you think Diane or Linda committed the crime?" *If Sandra and Joan are correct about a random suspect, Sam's answer should be no.* Serena watched, waiting to see his tail. Instead, his head appeared.

"Not fair, Sam." Serena shook her finger at him. "Maybe I should reword the question."

The red koi continued to stare at her. He seemed to say, "Think. Put my answers together."

"I've got it." Serena strolled along the fence, then came to a stop. When she looked down, Sam had followed her. "Sandra's evidence may point to the women. It will help me decide between Diane and Linda."

Sam leaped from the water and splashed Serena with droplets of water. "You heard something, Sam, because it happened here in the gardens."

Serena's phone pinged, showing she had a text message. "It's Sandra. She wants to meet in the gardens at eight a.m. tomorrow." She gazed down at Sam. "You are one heck of a fish, Sam. Don't ever change."

Chapter Seventeen

"Joan and I like to stroll through the gardens. It calms the spirit," Sandra said. "We found a quiet spot where no one could easily find us, if you know what I mean."

"We certainly do," Serena answered, glancing at her two friends. Despite thinking she knew every nook and cranny of the gardens, Serena was surprised to discover a white padded bench in a cul-de-sac setting she hadn't visited. "Is this your secret hiding place?" She teased.

"Perhaps." Sandra smiled. "The day after Amber's death, we came here seeking peace and tranquility. The plants and flowers distracted us from our worries. Joan is an avid gardener and tried to guess what they were. We spotted a statue tucked away in the landscape had fallen over. I wanted to fix it, so I reached for the little pagoda and before I could set it upright, I noticed something protruding from the dirt. I knew it didn't belong there, so Joan dug it out while I steadied the statue."

"Is it still there?" Lily asked.

"Yes, we put it back."

"Could you please show us?" Lily widened her eyes at Serena.

"Underneath here." Sandra touched the pagoda, but let Lily dislodge the item.

"It's a security badge," Lily said, shaking dirt from the plastic rectangle. "Identical to the one I need to get into the office downstairs."

"See," Sandra replied. "*That* woman killed Amber. She panicked, hid her badge and ran."

"What makes you think so?" Serena asked.

"Her name and picture are on it. Joan and I found it strange that an employee would bury her identification, so we went to the front desk and asked if we could speak with her," Sandra answered. "They claimed she didn't come to work that day."

"Was it her day off?" Mia asked.

"No, we asked the same question. She just didn't show up. That's when we got suspicious. What motivated this woman to bury her badge in the garden?"

Lily studied the card. "She has blonde hair like Diane or Linda."

"So?" Sandra shook her head. "You have another suspect. You need to find…" She looked over Lily's shoulder. "Marni Stern and interrogate her."

Lily tapped the badge against her hand. "I recognize her but have never spoken with her. Let me call downstairs and see what they say."

"Lily?" Serena pointed to the badge. "That could be evidence, especially if it has the killer's fingerprints on it."

"Darn!" Lily appeared upset. "What was I thinking? Anyone have a plastic bag?"

Serena always carried a bag of honey oat cereal for Sam. She took it from her purse and emptied the contents into a wastebin so Lily could drop the card inside. "It's the best I can do on short notice," she said, offering Lily the plastic bag. "We should get this to the police."

Lily took the bag from Serena while she waited to speak with someone in security. "Hey, Grady, Lily here," she said. "Is Marni Stern scheduled to work this week?" She went silent as she listened. "Is she a new hire? Okay, thanks." The expression on Lily's face said something didn't add up. "Marni is basically a new hire and has worked in security for five months. She is always on time and completes her assignments. Since Amber's death, she hasn't shown up to work."

"Strange." Serena nodded.

"You need to investigate this," Sandra demanded.

"True," Lily answered. "But why would Marni kill Amber? It makes no sense."

"I agree, but we must follow every clue." Serena reclaimed the bag from Lily. "I'll take it to the police station myself and insist they test it today." She faced her friends. "I might be there for a while. I'm staying until we get the results."

"Detective Bill will love that." Lily chuckled.

"Too bad. I'll bring Joan some lunch and keep her company. I'll become a permanent fixture if I must."

"I believe you," Mia said. "Anything you need us to do?"

"Let Jack and Tiger know the latest findings," Serena replied. "They were in Naples, Florida yesterday and might be in Columbus, Ohio, by now." She texted the valet to bring her car to the entrance. "Oh, one more thing. If the guys found anything, call me immediately. Any tip or clue, no matter how small."

* * * *

"Linda?" Surprised to discover the woman standing outside the hotel's entrance, Serena asked, "What are you doing out here? The police gave explicit instructions on where you can and cannot go."

"Oh, hi, Serena." Linda smiled. "I called the station and asked if I could visit Joan. They're sending a car for me unless you prefer to take me."

"I'm going there, too. Let me give them a quick call, and we'll be on our way."

"Never mind," Linda huffed. "I can wait." Her face brightened. "They sent me an email giving me permission to leave the hotel. I'm supposed to show it to anyone who asks." She flashed her phone at Serena. "Is this good enough? It proves I can leave the building."

"Fine. Get in." Serena pointed to her car parked by the front entrance.

"It's been such a long week," Linda said, sliding into the passenger seat. "My workload has doubled. I can't think about my job after what's happened, so I haven't logged on all week."

"I'm sure they'll understand," Serena replied, turning onto the street.

"Where do you live, Serena?" Linda asked.

"Out by the airport," Serena answered. "Why do you ask?"

"Just wondering about your commute. How long is it?"

"Depends on traffic, but usually under a half hour."

"I'd like to visit your home."

"What?" Serena glanced at Linda to see her aiming a small pistol in her direction. "Linda, put the gun down. You're not going to shoot me."

"Don't bet on that." Linda rolled down the window and shot straight up into the air.

"Are you crazy? That bullet could hit another car, or worse yet, a person!"

"I aimed for the sky," Linda said. "Just like I do in life."

"You killed Amber, didn't you?" Serena said as her phone rang. She saw Jack's name and realized he had important information. *I hope you discovered Linda is the killer. If you did, it's a little late for me.* She chastised herself for letting her guard down and believing Linda's story.

"Don't answer that," Linda growled. "Head for home, Serena. I mean it."

"Why?"

"You have two daughters who still live with you. I'm sure you want nothing to happen to them or leave them without a mother."

"You're threatening my daughters?" Serena's mama bear instincts rose to the surface. *Placate Linda. Protect your daughters.*

"I hope I don't need to go that far. You investigated the case and possess as much information as the police. I want to share my side of the story with you."

I don't believe her, but I'll play along. "Okay."

"Nina is rich, Serena, and I don't mean comfortable rich like Beth, Bonnie, Sandra or Joan. Suzanne, Nanette and Diane are stinking rich, but Nina has more money than that."

"So?"

"Nina can help me."

Serena pulled into her driveway and prayed no one was home. She took Linda into the house through the garage entrance. Linda tugged on her arm and said, "Introduce me as your friend."

"Mama? Girls?" Serena called.

"Oh, Serena, you're home," Robin said, coming into the kitchen. She spotted Linda and nodded. "Hello, to you, too."

"Mama, this is my friend Linda. She needed a break from the hotel, so I brought her here."

Robin approached Serena and embraced her. "I know," she whispered. "Jack called." She stepped away and smiled at Linda. "Can I get you something? Coffee?"

"That would be lovely."

"Please, sit." Robin gestured to the banquette. "I'll let you two talk while I make some coffee."

"Are Serena's girls home?" Linda asked. "I so want to meet them."

"They're at a friend's house," Robin answered. "A girls' sleepover before they head off to college. They should be home soon."

A shared glance between Robin and Serena conveyed volumes, a look only the two understood. Her mom had lied. Fortunately, Jack's timely call had saved the girls and gotten them out of the house. Serena drew in a long breath, her concerns now entirely focused on her mom.

For some strange reason, Serena's thoughts turned to the new book she hadn't started yet. *Secrets, Suspicion and Stolen Pearls* popped into her head as the perfect title. *Where's my journal when I need it? Why is my book coming to mind when my mom and I could possibly be killed? Because it's distracting me. Helping me think clearly. Obviously, Linda has secrets, so we'll start there.*

"Why did you steal the pearls, Linda?" Serena chose the safer topic of the two. *Going straight to the murder question may set her off.*

"This was the plan." Linda had chosen her seat well. She faced the kitchen, and no one could sneak up behind her since Serena had placed a fitted banquette in the nook. Appearing comfortable and eager to share her story, Linda said, "I'd take the pearls, send Nina a ransom note, get the money and return the necklace. A perfect plan."

"Okay, you did it for the money."

"Yes. I needed it."

"You live in an upscale neighborhood in the Columbus area, Linda. You and your husband still work. Do you need money that badly?"

"My husband drinks, Serena."

"That shouldn't deplete your resources."

"He gambles sometimes."

"That's tough. Have you tried to get him help?"

"He won't go. Says he doesn't have a problem."

"Did you try reasoning with him? Tell him you could lose your house and all the things you worked hard for?"

"We don't own the house. We rent from a family friend."

Linda's financial situation is becoming clearer, but it's still not a reason to steal and murder. "The only recourse you felt you had was to steal the pearls?"

"Yes, I had it mapped out to the minute."

"How did you get a key to Nina's floor?" Serena asked. "The front desk wiped them clean after you visited her apartment."

"I had a day to observe the inner workings of the hotel. No one noticed when I went missing. For all I know, the girls thought I was helping the cleaning staff." Linda scoffed. "Which I was, in a way. I tracked their movements in search of a daily schedule. Next, I watched the front desk staff and learned those employees keep in close contact with security."

"During this time, you stole a key from the front desk?"

"No, and I didn't steal it. I zeroed in on one woman. I believed she was a new security employee who they sent on more menial tasks. She visited the front desk several times in an hour. I borrowed her badge without her knowledge, of course. She fit the profile."

"Blonde hair and about your height. Age didn't matter," Serena replied.

"Correct. I followed her, hoping she would eventually visit the ladies' room. When she did, I followed her into the bathroom and accidentally bumped into her. While I was apologizing, I snipped the lanyard she wore around her neck. It fell to the floor as she headed to a stall, having no clue she had lost it. Her badge logged a person in and out of the security area."

I better let Jack know they need to upgrade the system. Yet this is just a hotel. I can see why they only issue a badge. "You went downstairs and made a key to Nina's apartment?"

"You can't make a key, Serena. You can only activate one. I had gone to the front desk, pretended I'd lost my room key, and they made me another."

"You activated one of those, but how? I wouldn't know where to start."

"You never asked about my occupation, Serena. I work for a security company that helps businesses find weaknesses in their systems so malware or pirates can't attack them. I know my way around a computer."

"What about the security cameras? You're an expert at those, too?"

"Not quite, but my son is. He has a small business that installs cameras in homes, stores and industry. I learned a lot from him. He offers other services, too."

"Such as?"

"Finding lost footage or repairing glitches."

"Let me guess. You worked for him and learned from the master."

"Exactly. Until two jobs became overwhelming, and I cut back to one." Linda looked toward the stove. "What is your mom's name?"

"Robin." Serena held her anger in check. "Why?"

"She needs to stay where I can see her."

"Mom?"

"I heard, darling. No need to worry, Linda. I won't do anything to make you use that little pistol in your hand." Robin approached, bearing a coffee carafe and a plate of cookies. She placed them on the table and retrieved two mugs.

"Oh, please join us, Robin," Linda said. She waited until Robin sat down with a cup of coffee.

"So now you have your key," Serena said. "Mia's fashion show ended, and the girls had made plans for dinner."

"Some of us wanted to rest or change. We agreed to meet in the bar at six. I chose a spot where they couldn't see me, and once they all arrived, I went up to Nina's apartment. I don't know how she did it, but Amber followed me."

"Knowing Amber, she probably had a key," Serena said. "We'll never know how she got one. They found nothing with the body."

Chapter Eighteen

"Speaking of Amber," Serena said as delicately as she could. "How did she end up dead in front of Nina's doorstep?"

Linda winced. "It was an accident, I swear. No one would believe me, so I ran."

"A knife in the back is no accident." Serena folded her arms over her chest.

"If you heard my side of the story, you'd agreed it was."

"We have time to hear it," Robin said, stirring her coffee.

"Fine." Linda rolled her eyes. "Having questioned Nina extensively the night before, I managed to locate her safe. It was easy to break in."

"Because you worked at a place where they taught you to do it." Serena couldn't help herself.

"No. I researched various home safes and how to open them when you lost the combination. After I retrieved the necklace, I ransacked her closet and left the safe open for dramatic effect. Make it look like a robbery. I wore gloves for the task but knew some prints should be found from our previous gathering." Linda narrowed her eyes. "That's when I heard her."

"Her? Meaning Amber?" Serena asked.

"Amber was pounding on the door. She screamed, 'I know you're in there, Linda. Let me in.' So, I did."

"Amber spoiled your perfect plan," Serena said. *Proving no plan is perfect.*

"She did. I panicked for a second but knew I could make it right. I would return the necklace to the safe and stage a failed robbery attempt. But Amber wouldn't help me. She felt Nina needed to know what kind of friend I was."

"Good for her," Robin said.

Serena widened her eyes at her mom, willing her not to speak.

"We stood in the foyer, and since Nina's apartment has an open plan, I spotted the block of knives on her counter. I wanted to threaten Amber. That's all. I headed for the kitchen, and she followed. When I grabbed a knife, Amber screamed, 'You are crazy! I am getting out of here. Nina will kick you out of the hotel, and Diane will expel you from the team.' I chased after her, begging her to listen. Amber opened the door just as I reached it. It caught my foot, causing me to stumble, and I lurched forward, unable to keep my balance." Tears rolled down Linda's cheeks. "When I got my bearings and sat up, I saw the knife had gone into Amber's back."

"Weren't you covered in blood?" Robin asked, appearing too interested.

"The blood soaked into my jacket, but Amber's dress absorbed most of it. I removed my gloves and jacket and went back inside to check for garbage bags."

"Nina has garbage bags?" Serena wrinkled her nose. "I just can't picture it."

"I discovered a box in a kitchen cabinet. Grabbing some paper towels, I wiped the knife clean before stuffing everything into the bag. I rode the elevator to the lobby, located a nearby wastebasket where I discarded the bag, erasing any traces of my actions."

Serena shook her head. *Did the police search every bin in the hotel? How could they?*

"I used the elevator to reach my floor and went to my room to change for dinner. While I was in the shower, I realized I couldn't keep the necklace or sell it."

"You set up one of your friends instead." Serena gave her a look of disgust. "Why Joan? Did she do something to you?"

"Her room was closest. I ran across the hall, knocked and dashed back to my room. Imagine my surprise when she went down to Sandra's room. It was the perfect opportunity…"

"To set her up." Serena finished the sentence. "You got away with it. Joan's in custody. Why do this?" She flung out her hands. "Hold me and my mom hostage?"

"I followed Sandra this morning. Last night, she couldn't stop talking about helping Joan and acted as if she had evidence to prove her innocence. When she took you into the gardens this morning, I panicked. I couldn't believe she found that darn badge. It was the perfect hiding spot."

"You heard our entire conversation this morning and knew your prints might be on the badge." Serena accused her. "I offered to take it to the station. In fact, the bag is still in my car."

"I couldn't remember how well I wiped it." Linda dropped her head and stared at her hands. "The original plan was to leave the card in the same bathroom so someone would find it, but I had to hide it until I devised my next move."

"So you buried it in the gardens," Serena replied. "What happened to Marni Stern? Is she…?"

"What? Oh, no. I overheard her on the phone in the bathroom. She'd gotten a call. Sounded like a family emergency. She mentioned she'd take a few days off and come home. I couldn't believe my good fortune."

"You're saying that Marni left the hotel and never called her supervisor. Lucky for you, she didn't notice her badge was missing."

"I can't say if she noticed or not, but it's the truth. Rushing from the stall, Marni assured the person not to worry. She would call into the office once she arrived home. Once the police formally charged Joan with the crime, and they gave us the okay to leave, I planned to return the badge to the bathroom." Linda met Serena's eyes. "Do you believe me?"

"It's quite the story. Isn't it, Mama?" Serena turned to her.

"Marni's story is too good to be true. Can you verify if this woman returned home or called into the office?"

"Lily could check," Serena answered. "But?" She tilted her head at Linda.

"It's fine. Call," Linda said.

"You'll allow me to make a phone call? There's more to this, right?" Serena raised her brow.

"Ask Lily to relay a message to Nina." Linda dug in her purse and produced a folded paper. She handed it to Serena.

Serena spread the paper out on the table and read the list. "Takeda private jet fueled and ready to take Linda to a safe location. Ten million dollars deposited into the account number provided. Send the Takeda limo to take Linda to the airport. Five thousand in cash ready for her use when she boards the plane. For incidentals, Linda?" Serena looked up from the paper. "Really?"

"There's one part I left out. You're coming with me."

"No!" Robin yelled. "Absolutely not."

"Mama. Serena placed her hand over her mother's. "It's okay. I'll go with her."

* * * *

"You are on speaker, Lily, so Linda can hear," Serena warned her.

"Okay, let me get this straight. Takeda jet. Ten million in an account. Takeda limo to drive you to the airport. Five thousand on plane. You're going with her."

"Lily needs to read the account number one more time," Linda said.

"I heard," Lily replied and read the numbers. "Is that everything? I'll get right on it."

"Thanks, Lily." Serena ended the call and turned to Linda. "Happy now?"

"It seems too simple. Lily was very business-like and agreed too quickly."

"That's Lily." Serena wished she could speak with her mom in private so she could say her friends were diligently working on a solution. All she could do was give Robin a smile.

"If you are going on a trip, let me fix you something to eat," Robin offered.

"I can't eat," Serena said.

"You will eat, Serena. I'll make your favorite. BLT."

"Bacon, lettuce and tomato?" Linda's eyes lit up. "I love those."

"Two BLTs coming right up."

"Mama, you don't…"

"I want to, baby." Robin touched Serena's shoulder as she stood.

Serena's phone rang, and she glanced at the woman across the table. "It's Lily. May I answer?" After Linda nodded, she said, "Lily?"

"Nina is working out the details. Please give her an hour. As for Marni Stern, Linda was correct. She apologized for leaving in such a hurry and not calling her supervisor. Her mother acted as if her father would die at any moment. Right now, he's resting comfortably in the hospital. In all the chaos, she had no idea she lost her badge until they told her."

"Thanks, Lily."

"Stay safe, Serena. Remember, you won't turn into a pumpkin at midnight."

"What does that mean?" Linda snapped. "It better not be code for something."

"No, it's just an inside joke we say to each other."

Tears burned the back of her eyes as Serena recalled the pressures of her last case. She had discussed her findings with Jack and was determined to solve it that day.

"Okay," Serena had said. "Let's get started. I've only got till midnight."

Jack pulled his brows together and had asked, "What happens at midnight?"

"I turn into a pumpkin."

"I highly doubt you could turn into a pumpkin." Jack had given her an inquisitive look and a quick kiss.

Later that night, Jack and Serena had ambled through the gardens after solving the case. They'd reached the pond and sat on the bench to finally relax. Jack then put a small rectangle-shaped black box in her hand. When Serena opened it, she gasped at the sight. A glass slipper, no more than three inches, shimmered under the lights. A ruby red gem, shaped like a heart, adorned the top of the shoe.

Jack pointed to the heart. "Your birthstone. July, right?"

"My birthday," Serena whispered.

"Yes, Serena, your birthday is this Saturday," Robin said, bringing her back to the present. "I'm baking your favorite cake."

Blinking away the memory, Serena looked at her mom. "I hope I get to enjoy it." She cast a glance Linda's way.

"You should be back by then," Linda said. "Once I land, you can fly home…unless I still need you."

After forcing down the BLT, Serena stared into her empty glass of iced tea. "Is it okay if I freshen up before we leave?"

"Where is your bathroom?" Linda asked.

"It's in the hallway." Serena gestured in the general direction.

"I'll come with you."

"Nature calling?" Serena asked in a sarcastic tone.

When they returned, Serena noticed her mom had cleared the table and sat waiting. "Your phone pinged, Serena," Robin said in a shaky voice.

"Thanks." Serena saw the text came from Nina. "It's Lily."

"Read it aloud," Linda demanded.

Go along with her plan. Serena read to herself, then said, "The limo will arrive in ten minutes." She set her phone on the table. "We should get ready. Since we don't know where we're headed, I have some coats in the mudroom. Would you like to bring them?"

"Show me."

After choosing two jackets, Serena led Linda to the front of the house. "We can wait here." She searched for her phone and realized it was still in the kitchen. "I left my phone on the table."

"Leave it," Linda demanded.

Serena kept repeating Nina's words in her head, which helped keep her calm. As they stood watching out the window, her mom slid in next to her and intertwined her fingers with Serena's. Serena gave her a quick squeeze, hoping to convey things would be fine.

Two bright lights blinded her for a moment, and Serena realized the limo had arrived. "I love you, Mama." She hugged her and whispered. "Do not come outside."

"I guess everything can't be sweetness and roses," Robin said under her breath.

Her heart lurched at the sentiment. Serena touched her mother's cheek. "I know."

"Let's go," Linda said, waving the gun toward the door. When Linda and Serena stepped onto the porch, two more cars pulled behind the limo. "I hope that isn't the police," she grumbled.

To Serena's surprise, eight women, including Nina and Joan, emerged from the cars. They congregated on the front lawn. The porch light flicked on, and Serena smiled. She knew her mom was watching from the window.

"What are you doing here?" Linda shouted.

"We came to reason with you. We are a team and want to support you," Diane answered, standing in front of the other women. "I know you, Linda. You didn't mean to kill Amber."

"You're right, Diane," Linda cried. "It was an accident."

"Tell your story to the police," Bonnie said. "Turn yourself in."

"No. They won't believe me." Linda shook her head. She grabbed Serena's arm. "Get out of our way."

Beth pushed through the group of women. "No. If you insist on going, take me instead. I started this, and I'd like to finish it."

"Beth, no!" Joan tried to stop her, reaching for Beth's arm.

"Back in college," Beth said. "I helped Amber. If I hadn't read Diane's planner and given the information to Amber, we might not be standing here today. I set everything in motion. Please, take me, Linda. Let me finish this."

Serena blinked back tears. "Thank you," she mouthed to Beth. *But it will not happen.*

"Nina doesn't care about you like she does Serena," Linda yelled.

"That's not true!" Nina exclaimed. "I care for them all."

"I'm done talking." Linda aimed the gun at the women. "Go back to the hotel, or…" She swung the weapon toward Serena, placing the gun in her stomach.

"Fine." Diane held up her hands. "We'll go. But first, may I ask a question? Why didn't you confide in me if you had money problems? I could have helped."

"Helped?" Linda laughed. "You viewed me like a puppy dog, always following your lead without protest. It was not an equal friendship."

"I'm sorry you feel that way," Diane said. "What if I came with you, and we could talk it out? I can help you now."

"Sorry, Diane. Too late."

"I believe Linda has said her piece," Nina replied. "Girls?"

As Nina turned, Serena caught a subtle tilt of her head. Serena glanced in the same direction and a car's interior lights flashed on. Parked two doors down, the dark SUV blended into the night. But when the lights turned on, Serena spotted Jack behind the wheel with Jade beside him. Jewel poked her head between the front seats so Serena could see her. *My girls are safe. Jack is protecting them.* Her heart swelled, ready to burst, as she finally released the tears she had held back all night.

Chapter Nineteen

"This is luxury at its finest," Linda said, settling into a cream color leather chair. "I never flew private before, and it's so exciting."

A handsome man with dark hair and a trim beard emerged from the cockpit. "Hello." He nodded. "My name is Chase Young, and I'll be your pilot. Mrs. Takeda chose her best pilot and co-pilot for this flight. Please inform the flight attendant if you need anything."

I know him. Serena searched her brain. *He's the husband of Mia's friend, Grace. Nina recruited him for the flight. I had no idea he was a pilot.*

When the flight attendant approached, Serena dug her nails into her palms so she wouldn't give him away. *Act natural. Like you never met him.*

"Hi, my name is Gabe. Can I get you anything?" he asked, pushing his black-framed glasses into place.

"Champagne would be nice," Linda answered.

"On its way." Gabe winked at Serena. "And you, miss?"

"Water, please."

"Certainly."

Serena watched Lily's husband walk to the front of the plane. Relief spread through her, knowing Nina had a plan in place. *Those men probably have their own weapons and won't let anything happen.*

"We should have asked the pilot where we're going," Serena said. "Let me get the attendant." She motioned to Gabe.

"Yes?" Gabe asked, taking a few long strides to reach her.

"Where will this flight land?" Serena asked.

"Somewhere in South America," Gabe answered. "I must speak to the pilot if you want more details."

"No, it's fine," Linda said.

"If it helps, we'll be in the air for at least eight hours," Gabe added.

"As long as there is food." Linda chuckled.

"I can bring you a cheese plate, if you wish."

"Sounds delightful. Thank you." Linda looked at Serena. "Such a kind and handsome fellow."

"He is." Serena dipped her head. *I'm going to have a little fun on this flight. If Nina stocked the plane, I'm going to see what they brought.*

Someone must have prepared the plate of meat, fruit and cheese ahead of time as Gabe returned in minutes. "There you go."

"By any chance, do you have cookies on board?" Serena asked.

"Wonderful almond ones from The Pearl's tearoom, ma'am." Gabe appeared to fight back a smile. "Would you enjoy a cup of oolong with them?"

"Not quite yet." Serena smiled, wishing to give Gabe a giant hug.

"You let me know." Gabe nodded and returned to his seat, where he could still see them.

"That sounds wonderful for later," Linda said, selecting a piece of cheese. "For now, let's enjoy this."

"Let's." Serena gave her a faux smile.

During their meal, Serena seized the chance to gather more information about the day Amber died. "You told me most of the story, Linda, but how did you sabotage the security footage? I understand you have the skills, but no one noticed you were tampering with the computers?"

"Marni Stern had blonde hair. It was the reason I followed her throughout the day and borrowed her badge. Once inside the security offices, I searched for her cubicle, but found nothing. Without an office, things became more difficult. I chose a desk, facing a wall, and waited until the shift changed or someone went to dinner. I needed access to a private office to work."

"Obviously, you got into an office."

"Yes. If everything had gone as planned, I would have returned the badge to the bathroom. However, as you know, I couldn't. The gardens seemed like the ideal burial place until the day I left the hotel."

"It didn't bother you that the police took Nina in for questioning?"

"She has enough money to pay for excellent lawyers. Nina never would have served jail time."

"How can you be so sure?" Serena's blood rushed through her veins to almost a boiling point, and she took calming breaths. "Then the police took Joan to the station, and you didn't feel guilty?"

"They would have eventually exonerated her. I hoped the police would let the rest of us go after they apprehended her."

"You made a few assumptions, Linda, which didn't work out in your favor."

"But look where I am now." Linda waved her hand from her chin to her waist.

Is this woman delusional? "You made it," Serena said. "Congratulations."

"To celebrate, I think it's time for tea and cookies," Linda stated. "Oh, Gabe?" She waved. "I could get used to this," she said with a smile.

* * * *

Serena woke to the sound of the captain's voice. "Please make sure you stay seated, and you fasten your seatbelts. We will land in ten minutes."

"We're here already?" Serena mumbled, not quite awake.

"You fell asleep," Linda said. "I dozed off, too."

They landed near the terminal, and Serena watched the crew roll the stairs into position. She wondered what would happen next. *Does Linda really get away with this? Nina surrendered so quickly. I hope she didn't do so on my account.*

Linda had stuffed her purse full of the provided money and now hugged it to her chest. "You get off first, Serena. Once you get on the tarmac, wait for me. You'll escort me into the terminal where I'll rent a car."

"Why didn't you have Nina provide a car?"

"I only trusted her to get me here. After that?" Linda lifted her shoulder.

Gabe opened the door and greeted the ground crew. He looked at the women and said, "We're ready, but I'm sorry. It's raining."

"We brought jackets," Serena said, grabbing her raincoat.

"Go on," Linda urged, flashing the gun. I'll be a few steps behind you."

This might be my only chance to tell Gabe the next step of Linda's plan. Chase stepped from the cockpit and nodded at Serena. "Thanks for the ride, Captain," she said. "And Gabe, you were wonderful."

"Watch your step," Gabe said, guiding Serena to the top of the stairs.

"She wants me to go to the terminal," Serena whispered.

"Don't worry," Gabe said under his breath. "Watch your step," he warned, raising his voice.

Serena took halted breaths, unable to think clearly. Dark, angry clouds filled the sky. Rain pelted against her jacket, and she struggled to see a few feet in front of her. She trusted the men, yet Linda's plan had gone too smoothly. *What if she makes me go with her?* She heard

Linda's footsteps behind her, but before she could turn to face the woman, Serena swore she saw a murky object coming toward the plane. *No, I'm seeing things.*

"Such handsome men," Linda said when she reached the bottom step. "I enjoyed the flight, but not this weather." She glanced around the airport. "I wonder where we are. It's so hard to see in this gloomy weather."

"Venezuela." A gravelly voice broke through the darkness.

The car's headlights turned on, and Linda gasped. August Morelli stood beside a black Mercedes under a black umbrella, which someone held over his head. The car door was open as if waiting for its next passenger. "I heard you're in need of a ride, Mrs. Gordon."

"Thank you, but no. I plan to rent a car."

"No need." August swept his hand toward the opening. "As you can see, we are ready to go. Now are you coming?" Two sturdy men, twice the size of August, came into the light. "Or do you need help?'

Linda grabbed Serena's hand. "Help me."

The rain had let up and intermittent drops fell onto Serena. Her heart pounded against her chest and her mouth went dry. She glanced up the stairs to see Gabe still at the top. He gave a slight nod which encouraged her to say, "I believe Mr. Morelli offered you a ride, Linda. I wouldn't turn it down."

"No! Please, no!" Linda cried. "I have money." She opened her purse as a gust of wind and rain blew across the tarmac and hundred-dollar bills flew into the air. "Oh, no."

"Leave them," August said, as Linda chased after a few bills.

Serena stood motionless as she witnessed the woman slide into the backseat. Her joints felt frozen, and she wondered if she could ever walk again. *Is this real or am I watching someone else's life unfold before my eyes? It's a movie. I'm asleep and dreaming. No, it's an out-of-body experience.* She shuddered, then felt soothing hands wrap around her shoulders.

"I got you," Gabe whispered.

Serena collapsed against his chest, unable to control her wobbly legs. "I'm sorry, Gabe. I can't…"

"No worries. Just breathe. It's over."

* * * *

After checking into the airport's hotel, Serena spoke with her family from the room's phone. She enjoyed how they kept talking over each other, asking questions, and reporting on events from home. Robin had put her phone on speaker, and Jade and Jewel gushed over Jack and how he devised the scheme for Serena to see them.

After finishing with her family, Serena called Jack. They talked for an hour, yet when she mentioned Nina, Jack said he hadn't spoken with her. Serena tried to call her friend, but she didn't answer. Finally, she gave up and went to bed, still curious about how August Morelli ended up in Venezuela. *Is Linda still alive?* Her nerves jangled at the thought.

Following a restless night at the hotel, Serena and the three men left for the airport. "I've never had this many handsome men escort me anywhere." She teased.

"Anytime." Chase tipped his captain's hat.

The co-pilot who managed the Takeda air services reminded her of Jack. Not in looks, but in demeanor. He was serious and all business, but when Serena made him smile, it brightened her day. She tried to get information from Gabe but only got cryptic answers.

"Nina wants to see me in person, right?" Serena finally asked.

"Perhaps." Gabe chuckled. "I'll tell you this. Lily and Mia can't wait to celebrate your homecoming. We're aware you want to get home but please indulge them."

"I will." Serena nodded. "I'll give them an hour."

Gabe sat with Serena on the flight home. Impressed by his story, she couldn't stop asking questions. "I feel like I really know you now, Gabe. A kid from Denver, Colorado achieves success, yet something is missing from your journey to the top."

"Lily."

"Right." Serena nodded. "You met in middle school, and she worked for you after graduating from college," she said. "I believe there's more to the story."

"There always is." Gabe chuckled. "It took a while to realize my true love was by my side the entire time. I was stupid."

"No, you weren't. You came to your senses." Serena patted his arm. "I love Lily, and as I get to know you, I believe we could be friends."

"Thanks. I'd like that."

Chase's voice came over the intercom. "You two ready to land?"

"Yes!" they exclaimed.

* * * *

Serena peeked out the jet's window to see Lily and Mia bouncing on their toes and waving to her. A limo sat on the tarmac, ready to take her home. Tears stung her eyes, and she turned to Gabe. "I didn't think I'd get this emotional."

"You went through a traumatic experience, Serena. I admire your courage and strength," Gabe said. "I'm going to help with the landing duties." He hopped from his seat and headed to the front of the plane.

Serena watched Gabe deftly open the door and speak with a ground crew member. He helped position the stairs, then waved to Serena. "Get ready," Gabe said. "There's two women who can't wait to see you."

"First, I want to thank you, Gabe. You didn't need to go on the trip."

"I volunteered."

"Same here," Chase said, emerging from the cockpit. He gestured to his co-pilot. "We all did."

"May I?" Serena held out her arms and walked toward the co-pilot. She gave him a gentle hug. "Thank you, sir." She turned to Chase. "You're next."

Chase returned the hug and said, "You're one heck of a woman, Serena Tate."

"Why thank you, Captain." Serena fluttered her lashes. "And you?" She pointed at Gabe, and he gave her the best hug, a bear hug.

"Come on," Lily shouted. "We need a hug, too."

Serena hurried down the stairs to her friends' waiting arms. They wrapped their arms around each other's waist and squealed in delight. *If I had to rate them, this group hug was the best of all.*

Chapter Twenty

"When we get inside, I need to find Nina," Serena said as the limo pulled up to The Pearl's front entrance.

"You will see her," Mia replied. "We're heading straight to the tearoom. After the lunch hour crowd left, Grandmother closed the restaurant to the public. No dinner tonight. We wanted to speak in private."

"So, Nina is waiting in the tearoom?" Serena asked.

"All questions will soon be answered," Lily said.

"I am glad we're here," Serena huffed. "I can't take much more of these non-answers."

After the trio walked through the Torii gate, Serena paused. "You go ahead. I'll be there in a minute." She waited until Mia and Lily were farther down the path before she approached the pond. "Sam, she whispered. "I'm back."

The water swirled in one direction, and bubbles formed on top. She waited for the koi to appear, but instead, Sam put on a show worthy of any paid experience she'd seen. He sprang from the water repeatedly and swam through the pond at lightning speed. What came next made Serena's jaw drop. More koi joined him in the acrobats and swimming show. She glanced around to see if other guests were enjoying the spectacular demonstration, but she stood alone. When it ended, Serena clapped for a full minute. "Wonderful, Samurai. Unbelievable."

It dawned on her no one *would* believe her, so Serena hurried down the cobblestone path to the tearoom, playing the show over in her mind. She smiled, knowing Sam presented her with a gift no one else could ever give her. "Maybe you're not real," she whispered. "But I sure hope you are."

When Serena arrived at the tearoom, Nina greeted her at the entrance. "It is good to see you, my child."

Serena burst into tears and slipped into the woman's open arms. "I knew you would save…"

"There, there." Nina patted her back. "Say no more. Come. Oolong tea is waiting."

Serena followed the woman to the table, wiping her tears with the tissue Nina handed her. Lily and Mia beamed as if they had a well-kept secret. She accepted a cup of tea after taking her seat. "I'm sorry," Serena said. "I didn't mean to cry."

"You have every right," Lily replied. "Just relax now and drink your tea."

"Okay." Serena chuckled. After a few sips, she looked at Nina. "I'm waiting to hear what happened behind the scenes."

"I've delayed it long enough, my dear. I wanted to see you in person and not hear it from anyone else," Nina said.

"Lily contacted me immediately after receiving Linda's demands. I didn't think twice about contacting Mr. Morelli for help. I told him I arranged for my private jet to take you and Linda to Venezuela."

"You always intended for me to go," Serena said in a surprised voice.

"There was no other way. Chase Young, a trusted friend, volunteered to captain the flight, along with James Ikeda, who oversees Takeda aviation."

"Gabe insisted on going," Lily said. "We were confident you would be safe."

"I felt very safe. Did Gabe have a gun?"

"No." Lily shook her head. "Only Chase."

"When I requested his service, August was more than willing to fly to Venezuela to greet Linda," Nina said. "Before I gave him flight details, we negotiated terms. He could scare her, but he had to bring Linda to San Francisco unharmed to face charges."

"Oh, he scared her alright," Serena replied. "His car came out from the cover of darkness, and when its headlights flashed on, it sent chills down my spine."

"Nothing happened to her, Serena. I promise," Nina said. "Mr. Morelli and I are in constant contact. When he lands, I'll notify the police, and they'll arrest her at the airport." She paused. "I have a surprise for you." Nina tapped on her phone and smiled. "Look over there."

Jade and Jewel walked out from the hall leading to the bathroom and private party area. They wore beautiful ruby red dresses and black heels, which took Serena by surprise. "They went all out, didn't they?" Serena laughed. The girls rushed to the table, and Serena leaped from her chair to hug them. "My babies!"

"Come with us, Mom," Jade said, taking her hand.

"Where are we going?"

"You'll see," Jewel answered.

The girls escorted her into the bathroom. "Well, maybe I need to…"

"Mom! Look." Jade pointed to a ruby red sequined mini-dress hanging from a hook in the outer powder room.

"It's gorgeous." Serena looked at Jade, then Jewel, and wrinkled her brow. "You don't mind if we match?" If Serena even wore the same color as the girls, they would change.

"No, put it on." Jade gave her a little push toward the dress.

"If you insist." Serena removed her shirt and jeans and slipped the cap-sleeve dress over her head. "It fits perfectly." She admired the look in the full-length mirror.

"We're not done," Jewel said. "You need shoes."

After sliding into a black high-heel sandal, Serena let out her breath. "Now am I good?"

"Almost." Jade opened the door. "Follow us."

The girls led Serena into the private party room and flicked on the lights. "Surprise!" a chorus of voices greeted her.

"What is going on?" Serena placed her hands on her cheeks.

"Happy birthday, Mom," Jade whispered.

"My birthday is Saturday," Serena insisted.

"But your party is today," Jewel said. "Enjoy. Look at everyone. Diane insisted on a dress code and required everyone to wear something ruby red in honor of your birthday because the ruby is your birthstone."

"Of course she did," Serena muttered.

Surprised by the birthday reveal, Serena was unsure where to turn or look first. She focused on Nina's friends, congregated in a group, and admired their attire. Some opted for elegant white dresses embellished with intricate red patterns or delicate floral designs. Others stood out in stunning ruby red dresses, including Nina, who evidently had found time to change.

Mia and Lily rushed up to her and linked arms. They, too, had changed into lovely red dresses. "Hope it's not too much," Mia whispered. "That Diane is quite the enforcer."

"No, I love it," Serena responded.

Lily and Mia guided Serena toward a wall where a white banner hung. It said, "Ruby Red Sweets" in large red script lettering. Towers of cupcakes with red or white frosting sat on the table along with cherry or strawberry covered cheesecakes. Heart-shaped cookies adorned with red frosting filled gold platters spread out among the towers of sweets. Bowls of raspberries, strawberries and red grapes also had a spot on the table.

A server offered Serena a glass of sparkling red wine, and she graciously accepted it. "How did you get this done in such a short time?" she asked her friends.

"We had many volunteers, Serena. The girls are dynamos," Mia replied, making air quotes when she said girls. "They know how to party. Take it all in." She waved her hand around the room.

Nina's friends had turned the space into a festive party room. Red, white and gold balloons adorned the dessert station. They had placed elegant balloon bouquets intertwined with red roses on tables draped in white linen.

Overcome by emotion, Serena's attention shifted to the assembled guests. Besides family and Nina's friends, she recognized familiar faces from the hotel, including her cherished friend, Jonathan, donning a striking red bowtie. Mai and Jun, their dedicated servers at the tearoom, raised their glasses in a heartfelt gesture when they made eye contact.

At long last, Serena's eyes landed on Jack. Her Jack. He stood with Kade and Gabe, who each wore ruby vests and ties over their white shirts. Black pants finished the look. She wondered if Diane had dressed them, too. She waited until Jack noticed her watching him. He lifted his head in greeting, excused himself and headed toward her.

Serena's heart sped up, and she couldn't contain herself. If she wasn't holding a glass of sparkling wine, she would fling herself into his arms and kiss him in front of all these people. "What the heck." She set the glass down on the nearest table and rushed toward him.

Jack appeared ready and opened his arms. He lifted Serena from the floor and spun in a circle as the guests applauded. "Hello, my love." He kissed her cheek.

My love. I'll take it. "Hello, to you, too." Serena gave him a quick kiss on the mouth. "We have so much to discuss."

"We do, but I believe Robin brought the karaoke machine you bought the girls for their birthday. We need to sing our song."

"Gosh, I hardly remember what we sang." Serena pretended to be confused.

"It was something about having the time of our life?" Jack wrinkled his nose.

The song began to play, and in an instant, the entire room began to sing. They gradually formed a circle around the couple, moving to the beat.

"This is the most wonderful birthday I've ever had," Serena cried, singing and dancing with Jack. "I don't want it to end."

* * * *

Well past midnight, Robin politely asked Serena and Jack to leave, even though she insisted on helping with the cleanup.

"We've got it, darling," Robin said. "It's your birthday. Enjoy time with Jack."

"I love you, Mama." Serena kissed her cheek. "Thanks for all you do."

"It keeps me young, Serena." Robin laughed and pointed to the exit.

Jack and Serena walked through the silent and empty tearoom, which was usually filled with people and the staff skirting around tables with their trays. Serena stopped and took a breath. "I love it here, Jack. Take in the calm. The tranquility."

"It is wonderful," Jack said. "I rarely come to the tearoom, but when I do, it's always crowded."

"Tonight, it's ours." Serena leaned against him and placed her head on his shoulder.

"Where's your favorite spot?" Jack asked.

"At our designated table." Serena pointed to the back corner.

"Let's sit. I'd like to give you a birthday present."

"Really?" Serena squealed like her kids did when presents appeared, but hoped it was only in her head.

Jack handed her a small white box tied with a red bow. He pulled his chair closer to Serena's and smiled. "I hope you like it."

Serena tugged on the ribbon and let it fall onto the table. She lifted the top and inhaled. "Jack, it's simple and beautiful. I love it."

A round red ruby set in silver hung on a dainty chain. It dangled from a card which read, "Love, courage and good luck."

"Is that what a ruby represents?" Serena touched the words on the card.

"The ruby not only symbolizes prosperity, but also embodies good fortune, courage and love."

"You did your research," Serena teased.

"Only for you." Jack appeared so serious Serena touched his cheek.

"You are one in a million, Jack Ando. I can't thank you enough for taking care of the girls while I went on my wild journey. When I saw you in the car that night, it calmed my spirit."

"I'm glad you saw us. I wasn't sure." Jack paused. "The girls wanted to show support. They begged to join Nina and her friends on the lawn, but I was afraid Linda might trade you for them."

"You did the right thing." Serena kissed him. "Thank you."

"When I landed at the airport, my only goal was to pick up Jade and Jewel from their friend's house. Nina messaged me, stating the limo for you and Linda would arrive soon. To keep the girls calm, I humored them by saying we were going on a stakeout. We parked a few houses down from yours and waited. When Nina and her friends walked onto the front lawn, the girls pleaded to be let out of the car."

"Child locks?" Serena chuckled.

"Yep."

"You called Mama when you couldn't reach me," Serena said. "You wanted to warn her about Linda after hearing from Nina."

"Yes, but obviously it was too late to stop her. Tiger and I learned Linda and her husband were in debt, and their upscale house in a Columbus suburb was a long-term lease. At the end of the year, it would have expired."

"Linda was desperate for money. Stealing Nina's necklace seemed like an easy fix," Serena said. "Her scheme might have worked. Hold the pearls hostage, and Nina would have paid."

"Linda may have devised the perfect plan, but as we learn in the business, something always goes wrong."

"I quizzed her, Jack, and asked about every detail leading up to the crime and afterward. Linda must have worked out the specifics months in advance."

"Hey." Jack gently placed his hand under her chin. "Enough shop talk. It's over. You found the killer. If Bill Mitchell had his way, Joan Fields would have gone on trial for Amber's murder. You never gave up, although things went sideways. I'm sorry I wasn't here for back-up."

"You took care of the girls, Jack. I couldn't ask for more." Serena took his hand from her chin and entwined her fingers with his. "Speaking of the girls, I have a great idea. I hope you'll volunteer to help."

"At your service," Jack said, coming in closer so they were inches apart. "How about you tell me later?"

Serena felt his breath on her skin and her breath hitched. She responded, "I highly agree."

Jack's lips found hers, and no further words were needed.

Chapter Twenty One

"Jade. Jewel." Serena took their hands and drew them into her office. "I have something to ask you."

"If it's something positive, the answer is yes," Jade replied.

"Did Jack ask you to marry him? I would definitely say yes." Jewel lightly clapped her hands.

"Yes, to Jade." Serena pointed to her daughter, then closed one eye and looked at Jewel. "And no, to you."

"What is it then?" Jewel asked.

"I promised to spend time with you before you left for college. As you know, something interfered with my plan. I will not begin my book, meet friends for tea or let anyone affect the remaining time we have together. I'm all yours." Serena spread out her arms.

"What about Jack?" Jade folded her arms.

"Did someone say my name?" Jack poked his head around the doorframe.

"Jack!" the twins exclaimed, gesturing for him to come in.

"Jack is here to help us with the project," Serena said.

"Mom, what project?" Jewel asked, tilting her head. "You better start talking."

"Look around." Serena waved her hand through the air. "I got to decorate my office and chose this color palette. Lately, it hasn't felt right. Something is missing. After I told Jack how I felt, he agreed. I want to look around and see my girls. Point to a lamp and say, 'Jewel chose that.' Walk on a soft rug and think, 'Jade insisted I buy this for my office.' Before you leave for school, I want your input on an office makeover. Out with the old. In with the new. We work together and make it a family project."

"I'd love to redo this space with something bold and daring," Jade said. Her eyes flashed with excitement.

"But that's not Mom, Jade. She needs a soft touch, too," Jewel replied.

"See? You're the perfect duo for the job," Serena said. "Bold and soft." She clasped onto their hands. "One favor. Do not tell Nina what I'm doing. She'll insist on paying. It's the reason Jack is here."

"I'm the handyperson, the delivery guy, and am available for any task which needs to be done." Jack's smile said it all. He was enjoying his role. "It's okay to boss me around."

Jade and Jewel giggled and retired to the sofa, already scrolling through their phones. They nudged each other when they found something, then agreed or disagreed. Serena knew they'd soon have ideas to present.

"What if I get everyone coffee?" Jack asked. He rattled off Jade and Jewel's orders as if he'd bought them every day. "Green iced tea, Serena?"

"Yes, thank you, Jack."

Serena sat watching her girls, heads together, laughing and smiling. She wanted to remember the moment, etch it in her mind forever. They had so much life ahead of them, yet at eighteen years of age, Serena had involved them in two murder cases. Still, their innocence shone through, clear and bright. *I must have done something right.* Her heart filled with pride and a thought overwhelmed her. *I don't need to worry about them at school. They'll do just fine.*

"Did someone order a skinny iced chocolate latte?" Jack asked. "I have a caramel one, too." He handed Jade the caramel and gave the chocolate to Jewel.

"Jack," Jade said in a deadpan voice. "You did that on purpose."

"Did I?" Jack turned to Serena. "Here is yours, my lady."

"Are we back in the nineteenth century?" Jewel teased, sipping on her correct latte now.

"Jack is having fun, girls. Let him be." Serena took the green tea and noticed he had one, too.

"Mom, are you ready?" Jade asked. "We've chosen a color scheme."

"I can't wait to hear."

"Navy blue walls, more like a dark blue, with white trim. A long light-oak desk will take the place of those counters and your smaller desk, along with a white chair of your choosing. Although we suggested a padded swivel one like this." Jade held up her phone.

Serena squinted to see. "Okay, I like it."

"Matching oak floating shelves on that wall," Jewel pointed to the right of Serena's desk. "And a brushed gold lamp on your desk. We'll work on decorating the shelves later. Photos of us are a must," she teased.

"You forgot the brushed gold geometric hanging lamp, Jewel," Jade reminded her, pointing at the ceiling.

"Sounds like I've got my work cut out for me." Jack chuckled. "We should paint first."

"And order these items," Jade added. "Mom, this is going to be fun."

"Flooring! Can we redo it, Jack?" Jewel asked.

Serena had beautiful chestnut hardwood floors. Examining the flooring, she said, "It would be a shame to remove this beautiful wood."

"We can sand and re-stain them," Jack replied. "Or I have a better idea. Keep them and cover them with a large rug."

"We'll find a cool one that you won't trip over, Mom," Jade said.

"I'll take no offense to the last part of your statement, Jade." Serena pretended to act insulted.

"Mom, you know what I mean." Jade rolled her eyes. "I have one question. How do we keep Nina from finding out? She walks past here to get to her office."

"I can answer that," Mia said from the doorway.

"Mia! Come and sit with us." The girls patted the spot between them.

"And tell me how Nina won't discover what we're doing." Serena stared at her.

"Grandfather finally came home last night. He's taking Grandmother on an extended vacation. One they both need. They plan to spend a week visiting friends in Oahu, then two weeks in Maui."

"It should give us enough time," Jack said.

"The real reason I came," Mia said. "Was to give you a message from Grandmother."

"Oh?" Serena leaned forward, eager to hear.

"The eagle has landed. Her code for Linda." Mia grinned. "Linda is back in the states and headed straight for jail."

"A sad ending to the reunion weekend."

"But they finally charged the correct person with the crime," Jack said. "Thanks to you."

"We all played a part in solving this one," Serena answered. "One more thing before we get back to decorating my office." She saw Jewel showing Mia their choices on her phone. "Mia?"

"Yes." Mia looked away from the screen and met Serena's eyes.

"Let's arrange a time to meet at the tearoom after Nina returns from her trip."

"Don't we always?" Mia giggled.

"Yes, but I promised to share something with you." Serena gazed at her, wanting Mia to remember.

"Nanette and Suzanne's nicknames!" Mia bounced on the sofa as the girls gave her a strange look. "Have you chosen a new loveseat yet? I'd love to help."

"We forgot about a sofa and chair," Jewel exclaimed. "So much to do. Jade, open your phone and let's get started. We've got three weeks to transform Mom's office."

Serena looked up at Jack, who stood behind her office chair. "We can handle this, right, Jack?"

"Compared to what we've been through?" Jack leaned down and kissed Serena's cheek. "It will be smooth sailing."

The End

Before You Go

Join Nancy's Mailing List and never miss a release!
Nancypennick.com

THANK YOU FOR READING

Did you enjoy this book?
I invite you to leave a review at your favorite book site, such as
Goodreads, BookBub and Amazon.

DID YOU KNOW THAT LEAVING A REVIEW...

Helps other readers find books they may enjoy.
Gives you a chance to let your voice be heard.
Gives authors recognition for their hard work.
Doesn't have to be long. A sentence or two about why
you liked the book will do.

Continue Reading –

The Pearl Hotel Cozy Mystery Series
(Cozy Mysteries are stand-alone reads)

The Model's Last Pose (Book 1)
Gone with the Pearls (Book 2)
The Notorious Nutcracker Case (Book 3)

Other Books by Nancy Pennick

The $ecret Billionaire $ociety
(Contemporary Romantic Suspense)

Chase (Book 1)
Nash (Book 2)
Finn (Book 3)
Beau (Book 4)
Gabe (Book 5)
Kade (Book 6)
The Elusive Mr. Smith (Book 7)
Smith's Revenge (Book 8)

The Billionaire's Bride
(Contemporary Romantic Suspense Series)

Vanessa (Book 1)
Grace (Book 2)
Charlotte (Book 3)
Tess (Book 4)
Lily (Book 5)
Mia (Book 6)

**The Clan MacLaren Series
(Historical Romance)**

My Highlander Husband (Book 1)
Donnach's Daughter (Book 2)
The Heart of the Emerald (Book 3)
Now and Forever (Book 4)
MacLaren Strong (Book 5)
Homecoming (Book 6)

ABOUT THE AUTHOR

For three decades, Nancy taught elementary school. She'd written short stories as a child, kept a diary and loved the writing process. After retiring, she hadn't set out to become an author, but when inspiration struck, she couldn't resist putting pen to paper. She now had time to follow her dream. Today her writing spans various genres, including young adult, historical romance, romantic suspense and cozy mysteries.

Nancy lives with her husband, Ron, and has a married son, who helps her with tech more than he likes! Plus, add in a wonderful daughter-in-law and grandson which makes her life complete.